The Binmen are Coming

by

Louis Graham

Cover Design and Illustrations by the Author

First published 1988 by Countyvise Limited, 1 & 3 Grove Road, Rock Ferry, Birkenhead, Wirral, Merseyside L42 3XS.

Copyright © Louis Graham, 1988.
Photoset and printed by Birkenhead Press Limited, 1 & 3 Grove Road, Rock Ferry, Birkenhead, Merseyside L42 3XS.

ISBN 0 907768 21 0

To Frank and Freda with love.

CONTENTS

Chapter 1

THE LOWEST RUNG

Three million unemployed and I was one of them, yet it was a full time job trying to get work. Every day I'd gone to the job centre. I'd written letters, attended interviews, in fact every conceivable avenue in my range I'd explored. All to no avail!

Getting a bit desperate, I thought of lowering my sights to the very bottom. I was going to try being a binman and you couldn't get lower than that!

Bright and breezy I went down to the job centre. Marching up to the girl sitting behind the desk I said "Good morning, I'd like to be a binman."

Laying her pen down and leaning back in her seat, she gave me a smile "Well well, what driving ambition you have, but I'm afraid you'll have to start lower down the ladder."

My mouth dropped open "You mean there's a position *below* that of binman! I don't believe it, I thought that was the bottom rung!"

She looked indignant "Binman is a good job. You'd have to start as a street sweeper though, that's the lowest. You then work your way up."

"Well" I said sarcastically, "what qualifications do I need?"

Picking up her pen and rolling it round her fingers she gave me another smile "Surprisingly, you do need some. You have to be able to read and write."

"To sweep the streets and empty dustbins?" I asked her in disbelief.

"Think about it," she retorted, holding up the pen "if you couldn't read or write, how would you fill in your time sheet? Also, how would you return the empty bin to the correct house if you were unable to read the number on the bin or the back gate?"

Scratching my head, I said "I am surprised, I'd never ever thought about it like that! I have passed the C.S.E. Do you think that would qualify me to sweep streets?"

Her smile developed into a laugh "No not really, you will need something else!"

"Good grief" I said "I think I'll try something simpler, like a top executive position!"

"Now don't be like that!" she said, laying her pen down with a crack.

"Alright I'm sorry, but what do I need? Another twelve months in school to be a street sweeper?"

"No that wouldn't be necessary, I think you could pass the I.Q. Test O.K."

"Are you kidding me?" I asked her, trying to determine if she was serious or just having some fun at my expense.

"No I'm not!" she said, looking me up and down "It's the physical side of it I'm thinking about. You'll have to be fairly fit as well. For example, would you be able to empty hundreds of bins every day and keep on week after week?"

"Are you trying to put me off? Does anyone ever get a job as a binman?"

She looked serious now as she replied "I'm just being very careful, because some men that I've sent down to the yard have only lasted one day on the bins! If you think you have the stamina for it, I can give you a green card. A vacancy just came in for a street sweeper this morning."

Things were beginning to look up. "Thank you very much" I said "I'd like to try it, a job of any kind these days is something."

Handing me a green card, she said as pleased as punch "Go down to the yard and ask for Mister Carson at the Cleansing Department, he's the Cleansing Inspector. Binmen and street sweepers come under his jurisdiction."

"Thank you very much." I said, taking the proffered card and stowing it safely in my pocket.

The girl smiled saying "I hope you're successful in your chosen profession."

"Thanks, but I haven't got the job yet."

She bent her head and started writing again and I barely caught her final words "There's no doubt that you'll get it. They'll take almost anyone down there!"

I looked at her sitting there pleasantly smiling, and just couldn't take umbrage at her last remark. By her expression I didn't think she meant anything by it anyway.

"Thanks for everything." I said, heading for the door and my new career.

The borough yard was on the other side of town and having plenty of time on my hands, I walked all the way. It was the middle of June and the day was beautiful. Anyway I needed the exercise to get me ready for the heavy job that I might be getting soon.

Walking through the yard gates, I stopped the first person I met. "Excuse me please, can you tell me where I'll find the Cleansing Inspector?"

Looking down at me, he rolled his eyes and then spat on the ground about two or three inches from my right foot. "You want Mister" — he spat again — "Carson!"

Sneaking a look to see if my shoes were still dry, I said "Yes, that's right."

Lifting a calloused hand he pointed up the yard "Go to the end of the yard, on the right you'll see an office block, the Bear'll be in there, sitting on his fat backside!"

Thanking him, I made my way round the sputum and headed for the offices. Going through the main door, I found one marked 'Cleansing Inspector'. I knocked, and a deep voice bellowed "Come in."

Opening the door and walking through, I was confronted by a heavy set man with a bushy moustache sitting behind a large desk.

"I'm looking for Mister Carson." I said, trying to drag my eyes away from his hairy eyebrows, which were two miniature versions of his moustache.

The moustache waggled and the sound came from somewhere below it. "You've found him, what can he do for you?"

"I've come from the job centre." I replied, handing him the green card.

"Good" he growled, motioning to a chair "have a seat."

Without taking my eyes off the hairy bear-like face I eased myself into the empty chair on my side of the desk.

"The girl at the job centre said that you have a vacancy for a street sweeper."

"That's right" he said, his moustache waggling with every syllable "but we call the position, street sweeper stroke binman."

"What does that mean?" I asked, wondering if binmen were prone to strokes!

One eyebrow went up and the moustache growled again "Well, if a binman is sick and doesn't turn in, where do you think we get a replacement from?"

Feeling a bit silly, I replied "Presumably a street sweeper takes his place."

He glowered at me with a look that said 'I'm dealing with a moron here' but aloud he said "That's right, you've got the picture. So street sweepers don't go out the yard in the morning until all the bin crews are filled. When you come in you won't know whether you'll be on the bins or the brush!"

"That's fine, I'm willing to do anything." I said, trying to show him how enthusiastic I was.

"Could you manage to lift heavy bins for eight hours every day?" he asked, his other eyebrow going up this time.

"Yes, I'm sure I could. You know, that's just what the girl in the job centre asked."

I watched fascinated as his eyebrows closed ranks and went up together "Well she may ask that," he growled "she's been sending a few puny ones down lately!"

"I think I could manage, I'm fairly strong." I said holding up my right arm and flexing my bicep.

He completely ignored that and asked "Are you a good time keeper?"

"Yes," I replied, holding up my watch in an effort to try and impress him.

His eyes rolled upwards, showing his exasperation "I know your bloody watch'll be a good time keeper," he spluttered "but what about you?"

"N-n-never late. Always on time!" I stammered.

"Alright, do you have a driver's licence?"

I laughed "Why, do your hand carts have engines?"

When his eyebrows started to dance I knew that I'd said the wrong thing.

11

I couldn't see his mouth moving under the moustache, but it must've been because he said "I see by your card your name is Mackenzie."

"Yes, it's Steve Mackenzie." I said in verification.

"Well, Mister Mackenzie" he continued "we're overstocked with comedians in this depot, we don't require any more!"

Now I could see even this menial job vanishing before my eyes. "I'm really very sorry" I said imploringly "but I thought that binmen were jocular people."

"Yes, but you're not a binman yet! By the way one of the sweeper's carts has an electric motor and you need a licence for it!"

With a pleading look I said again "Again, all I can say is, I'm sorry, I shouldn't have made that remark."

The Bear's expression seemed to change. Shuffling his feet under the desk then scratching his head, he said "We may have a problem in the near future."

That remark seemed vague "Would that involve me?" I quizzed, getting into the eyebrow game by raising my right one in puzzlement.

He spread his hands "If you take this job, it certainly will!"

Feeling elated now that I might get the job but puzzled at what he was getting at, I asked "What do you mean?"

Leaning back and folding his arms, he replied "There's very strong rumours that the Cleansing Department is going to go private. So if I give you a start, you could be made redundant quite soon. It could be a couple of years or it might be just a couple of months! Nobody seems to know when, but it seems that it is certain!"

"Good grief" I said "I'm getting the sack before I start!"

"Jock, do you want to try it? When the private firm takes over, they might keep you on."

"Yes, I'll take it. At least it'll be a few month's work."

"Alright, start tomorrow morning, seven forty five sharp."

"Thanks very much, I'm grateful but tomorrow is Thursday!"

The Bear's eyebrows rose once again "So! Don't you work on Thursdays?"

"Yes of course I do" I said, thinking that I'd put my foot in it yet again, "but I thought everyone started on Mondays."

His eyes bored into me "Jock, when you start work tomorrow you can stop thinking. I'll do the thinking for you!"

"Yes sir." was all I could say.

He laughed "Call me Jim, I'll see you tomorrow, Jock."

Chapter 2

FIRST DAY

In the morning I was at the yard in good time. Looking around I picked someone that appeared to be a street sweeper. At least he had the characteristic slow walk of one, and had his hands stuck deep in his pockets.

"Excuse me" I said, reducing my speed to match his "where do street sweepers report?"

He didn't even break step. Plodding on, he countered with his own question "New start?"

With the same brevity, I replied "Yup."

He nodded towards a building on our right "Bear's in the messroom."

That scintillating conversation concluded, I made my way to the designated door. When I walked in, the first impression was of an opium den. The murmur of voices was low, probably because the sound couldn't get through the thick pall of blue cigarette smoke.

"Good morning." I said to all the vague shapes that were sitting around.

A Welsh voice came out of the gloom "Bloody hell, we've got another Haggis!"

"Haggis tastes better than flaming leeks!" I retorted in the same tone as my hackles rose.

"Goodonyer!" another voice said, the owner obviously not being a confederate of the Welshman in the corner.

The Bear, Mister Carson, was sitting at a table with a large sheet of paper in front of him, ticking off names as men came in.

As I approached the table the Bear looked up. "Reporting for duty, Mister Carson." I announced, wondering if I should stand to attention.

The eyebrows went up and the moustache quivered "I'm not blind, Jock! Sit down!"

I took a seat at one of the tables.

An old fellow wearing a corduroy cap stained with years of gunge sat opposite me. He took a long draw at his cigarette, formed his lips into a little circle and exhaled slowly, adding to the haze. When it was all out, he said "Where do you come from, Haggis?"

"Orginally, do you mean?"

"Yeah, where about in Scotland do you hail from?"

"South west" I replied "Ayrshire, to be exact."

Andy Cap looked interested, he blew out another cloud of smoke and between coughs asked "That's Rabbie Burns country, isn't it?"

"Yes it is." I confirmed, as I tried to shallow breathe in an effort to lessen my smog intake.

"Do you know any of his poems?" Andy continued.

"Yes, I could give you a few stanzas if you'd like to hear them."

He held up his hand "Not in here Haggis, this lot wouldn't appreciate it. Most of them never get past page three in the paper!"

A large guy with a cowboy hat sitting at the next table, rolled his cigarette to one side of his mouth and butted in "Listen to Andy Cap! Don't take any notice of him Haggis, he's got more dirty books in the cab than anyone else!"

Andy Cap looked hurt. With a pained expression, he asserted "It's the artistry I'm interested in!"

The roar of laughter that greeted that remark told it's own story.

The messroom was gradually filling up. All the seats were taken and men were standing around talking. The air was so blue with smoke that you didn't need to have a cigarette to get nicotine poisoning! The only thing bluer than the smoke was the language. It was purple and overripe!

The Bear looked up "You got a full crew, Frank?"

"Yeah!" Came the affirmative from the ganger.

"On your way then!"

With a bit of scuffling and scraping of chairs, six men rose and went out the door. Their driver was waiting in the wagon with the engine revving. Then with banging of doors and a lot of shouting, they were off with a roar.

Scanning the remaining men, the inspector's eyes finally rested on Sam, the charge hand of round two "You're waiting for one!" he growled, making it a statement rather than a question.

Sam replied nevertheless "Yeah, Slim's not in yet."

One of the sweepers lounging at the window, proclaimed "Slim's coming now and he's been on the randan last night by the look of him!"

"He won't be fit for very much then, and he's trucking this week!" grumbled Sam, pulling a face.

"What'you waiting for? You've got your crew!" growled the Bear.

The gang from round two got up and stormed out to their wagon.

Examining his sheet closely then lifting his head, the Bear sighted on the Cowboy and fired the question "You still want one?"

It ricocheted — "Yeah, we do. Can you give us one of the sweepers?"

The Bear barked at a guy standing by the toilet door "Tell the Beak he's on three!"

The fellow banged on the door, shouting "Come on out Beak, you're on round three!"

Muffled cursings came from behind the door, then it burst open and out came the Beak like a hurricane!

I saw the reason for his nickname. His nose was long and pointed, making him look like an eagle.

"Why should I go on three?" he bellowed "That round's the last!"

"Three has top bonus." the inspector announced calmly.

"Stick the bonus!" snarled the Beak in a vitriolic manner.

Glaring at his opposer, the Bear drew his eyebrows together and barked "Round three or you're shovelling sand!!" The words coming out like machine-gun bullets.

"B-----!" — "I'll go on the bins!" snarled the Beak, kicking the door on his way out.

Grinning at the charge hand, the inspector said "There you are Cowboy, a good willing worker for your gang!"

"You *must* be joking!" Cowboy spat out.

"If he gives you any trouble, send him back and he can go home. There are plenty of men on the dole eager to work, so don't stand any nonsense!"

Cleansing Inspector – the 'Bear' being bearded by the 'Beak'.

"O.K." the Cowboy said, then turning and beckoning with his arm to the men, drawled "Wagons roll, boys,"

With a clatter, the last bin gang left the messroom.

Looking round the room from man to man, the Bear's eyebrows went up one at a time "Well well," he said "what have we got left? — The dregs of humanity!"

There were four of us left in the messroom, obviously four street sweepers. A young lad with gold rimmed spectacles was scowling at the Bear. He swallowed hard and spoke up "Mister Carson" he said as he shuffled his feet "I object to being called the dregs of humanity! I'm a student. This job is only temporary."

This sort of situation was right up the Bear's street. He sat and looked at the boy for a few minutes without saying anything. We all fell silent.

The Bear leaned back in his chair and folded his arms. "What are you studying, lad?"

The student was now the focus of attention "Fine arts." he replied proudly.

"Fine arts" repeated the Bear, rolling the words round his tongue. "Very good! Well I'll give you a *fine* job. Go to the sweepers' shed, get a wheel barrow, brush and shovel. Go down to the prom and shovel fine sand from the prom back onto the beach. Keep at it all day! I'll be down at dinner time to see how you're getting on."

Aghast, the student croaked "That's not fair, Mister Carson!"

The Bear seemed thoughtful "You're right! One day isn't long enough to get used to it. You can go back on sand tomorrow again!"

The student was speechless!

"Anything else?" queried the inspector, knowing that there wouldn't be.

He was right. The lad muttered "No" and walked out.

Turning his head, the Bear focused on another sweeper. He then looked at a pile of cards in front of him, selected one and handed it to the waiting sweeper "Here y'are Skinny, it's round four, day three!"

Skinny took the card, shoved it straight into his pocket without looking at it, said "Ta" and marched out the door.

Rummaging through the rest of the cards, the Bear picked one out and handed it to me "Here y'are Jock, you've got a nice one, round five, day five!"

18

Gathering up his things from the table, the Bear stood up and moved toward the door. Before he reached it, the last sweeper piped up "What about me, Jim?"

As he grasped the door handle he turned to face the old sweeper "You go with Jock today Tom, and show him the ropes."

The four of us went to the sweepers shed. While Tom was getting the hand cart ready, with our brushes and shovels, I looked at the card.

There were about twenty streets on the card. Half of them were marked 'sweep' with a time in minutes against each one. The other half had 'patrol' against the names of the streets. I totted up all the minutes marked on the card. They totalled seven hours thirty minutes.

All the gear was on the cart and old Tom clanged the lids shut.

"Tom," I said "these streets on the card are on the other side of Hoylake. They're about two and a half miles away. How do we get there?"

He laughed "We walk, Haggis, we walk pushing our little cart!"

I looked at him in amazement "That's impossible Tom, the card says we need seven and a half hours to do the work!"

"So what's your problem?" he asked as he adjusted the brush that had fallen off the cart.

Tapping my watch, I said "Look at the time now, by the time we get there it'll be at least nine o'clock! We'll be about an hour and a quarter behind time before we even start!"

Tom went into a kink with laughing. When he recovered he said "We'll be more behind than that, Haggis, because when we reach our territory it'll be time for our tea-break!"

I shook my head "The whole thing's crazy!"

"It's the system Haggis, don't worry about it." he said in a tone as if he were trying to console my conscience.

The Bear marched round the corner "You bloody lot still here" he raged "if you don't move your arses fast, you'll all get an n.b.e.!"

We got out the yard as quickly as possible and set off for our designated streets. I felt a right charlie pushing the little green cart along Market Street. It looked like a pram, but felt as if I was trying to push a Sherman tank. By the squeals and squeaks it sounded as if a little bit of oil wouldn't go amiss.

19

A lout standing in a doorway shouted "What have you got there, twins?"

"I'll give you twin black eyes!" I shouted back.

"Where'll you get a bloody army in a hurry?" retorted the lout.

We ignored him and carried on walking.

"Tom" I said loudly, trying to make myself heard above the squeaking of the cart "what did the Bear mean when he said we might all get an n.b.e.? It sounds like an award."

I thought he was going to go into another kink, but this time he managed to control himself. Amidst chuckles and coughs he said "You could call it an award. The initials n.b.e. stand for: *no – bonus – earned!*"

"Good grief." I said "The pig!"

"Not a pig, Jock. A bear! And wait till he gets a sore head!"

Sighing, I said "Alright Tom, let's get mobile, where do we start?"

"School Lane, at the bowling green." he replied without any hesitation.

I stopped, dropped the cart on it's rear wheel and took out the card. "You've made a mistake Tom, that's not on our list."

"No mistake Haggis," he chortled "we take our tea-break in the green keepers hut."

Shoving the card back in the cart, we resumed our march.

"Hell's bells," I said "my first tea-break and I haven't done a stroke!"

"You worry too much, Haggis. You've pushed this cart for a couple of miles. That's work, isn't it?"

I was beginning to get a bit winded "It certainly is! We'll need to get some oil on these wheels when we get back."

"Yeah, we'll do that."

We arrived at the bowling green. The green keeper wasn't around, but the hut was open. So with Tom leading the way we went in and sat down at the table.

"Do you want some tea from my flask? It'll save you making any." I asked him as he unwrapped his butties.

"No thanks Haggis, I've got a flask here in my bag."

Tom lifted one of his butties and opened it. He gazed at the filling with a look of disgust on his face, then slapped it down on the table with a loud bang that made me jump.

"Bloody cheese again!" he grumbled.

With my hanky I mopped up the tea that had slopped over the edge of my mug with the bang on the table.

"I take it you don't like cheese." I remarked, stating the obvious.

"Hate the stuff!!" he grated through clenched teeth.

Looking at him in surprise, I said "The solution's easy, tell your wife to put something else on them."

He had started eating and through a mouthful of cheese, he murmured "I'm not married!"

There was a silence as we both got through our first butty. When I had swallowed the last mouthful, I asked "Who makes them up?"

His face expressionless, he replied "I do."

Another short silence while I digested this remark. I took a look at his face to see if he was having me on. It was dead-pan!

"Why then in heavens name do you put cheese on your butties if you don't like it?"

He looked at me as if I were stupid "Cheese is very good for you. It's very nutritious, what do you think has kept me going all these years?"

"There are other things besides cheese." I said, chomping a lump of corned beef.

"Like what?"

"Corned beef, it's just as nutritious as cheese." I assured him. "The British nation lived on it during the war."

His brow furrowed "Yes, but have you seen the price of it? I'm only a street sweeper, you know!"

"Give me one of yours Tom, and I'll give you a corned beef one."

We exchanged butties.

I opened it up and looked with horror at the thick piece of red leather stuck there in the middle.

"Good grief Tom, it's red stuff." I lamented, then shut my eyes and took a bite. "No wonder you don't like cheese, you could sole your

21

boots with this! Why don't you get something else? A good white cheese, Lancashire or anything like that. It would be preferable to this red rubbish!"

"Is the white stuff better?" he asked as he devoured my corned beef butty.

"Chalk and cheese!" I replied, then tried to wash down the red leather with strong tea.

"I might try that" he said, picking up a morsel of corned beef that had dropped and shoving it in his mouth "but I've always had red cheese."

"You are allowed to change."

"O.K., you've made your point" he said resignedly "I'll get some Lancashire cheese tomorrow."

Our butties consumed, we poured ourselves another cup of tea and Tom took out a battered old pipe. It took four matches to get it under way.

I looked on fascinated "Where on earth did you get that thing, Tom?"

Taking a few more puffs to make sure it was going well, he took it out his mouth, held it up and said "This pipe will be much older than you, Haggis!"

"I don't doubt that!" I said with a chuckle, as I looked at him sitting there like an old fashioned Popeye. "I bet it was you that was causing most of the smoke in the messroom this morning."

Puffing contentedly at his short-stemmed old pipe, he was quickly engulfed in a pall of smoke "That's my motto, Haggis!"

"What's that, 'smoke everybody out'?" I asked with a cough.

Exhaling a cloud of thick smoke he said "No, it's share and share alike! I like everyone to get the same enjoyment that I do!"

Turning up my nose I said "Is that what you call it? Anyhow Tom, tell me about the cleansing department going private. What's happening, exactly?"

He took the pipe out of his mouth and poked into the stem "Don't rightly know, Haggis. Everbody's on the qui vive, not being sure if they have a job or not! In the old days being on the council was a job for life. Not now! Times are changing!"

"How will they work the redundancies? Will it be last in, first out?"

22

He laughed, and had a good cough. When he'd recovered he said "No it isn't. It's privatization! That means a private firm takes over, so *all* the cleansing staff get the boot!"

"Ah well", I said, getting up and washing out my cup in the sink "if I get a couple of months work it'll be something."

Tom knocked out his pipe "Work! Yeah that reminds me, we'd better go and do a little of that now!"

We got our cart and headed for the streets marked on the card. Tom pushed it along as I looked at the list of streets.

"Tom, I've been looking at this card and I think that it's impossible to do all the streets in the time they've got down here. We could never earn top bonus."

"We can Haggis, no problem!" he said as he chewed on the end of his unlit pipe.

"How?"

"We use psychology?"

"Have you ever been psycho-analysed, Tom?"

"No, I don't believe in it. People who go to a psychiatrist need their heads examined!"

"You're having me on" I said, looking to see his expression "that's a contradiction!"

Without missing a step he balanced the cart with one hand, took the pipe out of his mouth and gave a nice ripe tobacco spit on the road "It's not, Haggis. Psychology and psychiatry are different. What we use is applied psychology."

I was still puzzled "How do we do that?"

"Well, look at it this way, how do you think our bonus is gauged?"

Thinking about it for a minute, I replied "I suppose if the inspector sees that our work is alright he'll mark our bonus accordingly."

Taking the pipe out of his mouth again, he said "That's exactly right." Then with a well aimed spit, scored a direct hit with a resounding ping on an old beer can lying in the gutter. "Will you pick up that can, Haggis?" he added.

Picking up the can gingerly, opening the lid and throwing it in the cart, I said "But we still can't do all the streets in the time!"

"That's true, but the Bear's a busy man and he hasn't time to examine every street. He goes to head office every day along the main drag. As he passes he looks up all the streets we're supposed to have swept."

"So where does the psychology come in?"

He chortled "Simple, Haggis. We brush all the corners of the streets that he can see. If things look tidy as he passes he doesn't worry too much. There'd be no sense in doing most of the streets and leaving some of the ends that he sees, dirty!"

I was astounded "Well well, I didn't know that I'd need psychology to earn bonus sweeping streets!"

"There's a lot more to it, Haggis. You'll learn as you go along."

"You've been at this game a long time Tom, how old are you?"

Laughing, he replied "Don't rightly know, I'm thinking of cutting off one of my legs and counting the rings!"

I retorted "I'm going to be on the pension before we get started!"

He stopped suddenly and the cart rattled to a halt "Don't worry, Haggis! We're here, this is where we start."

Eagerly I lifted a brush off the cart "Do we sweep this first one Tom?"

"No, just ignore the card where it says 'sweep'!"

"O.K." I said "What about the next one on the card? It's marked 'patrol'! What does patrol mean?"

"All that means Haggis, is that we walk up the street and pick up any pieces of paper or any other muck lying around, but it's best to ignore the whole card!"

I threw the brush back on the cart "Good grief Tom! Do we just go home and wait for our wages to be delivered?!"

With the perpetual twinkle in his eye, you couldn't tell whether he was serious or just having you on. He laughed, "No," he said "if you look along you'll see six streets coming off this one. You go along with the brush and sweep the ends of each one. Go into each street for about twenty yards only. Leave the sweepings in little piles. I'll come behind you and pick them up."

It took us about an hour to do the lot. When he caught up I said "What now?"

He sat on the cart and started filling his pipe "We go back for lunch." he said, striking a match on his boot. I watched fascinated as

24

his cheeks hollowed in a valiant effort to puff his old pipe into life.

Looking at my watch, I remarked "But it's only just turned eleven. Lunch is twelve o'clock, isn't it?"

The amount of smoke indicated that his pipe was now well alight, and with a lit pipe, Tom was even more of a sage. He puffed contentedly, gazed at me with critical concern, then trying to blow a smoke ring but not quite succeeding, he said "Haggis, slow down! If you don't you're going to take a heart attack! What's the use of medals on a shroud?"

"That may be so, but surely we're not going to sit here till dinner time?" I protested.

"Take it easy, everything's worked out! As we go back, we walk slowly through these other four streets that can't be seen from the main road. We pick up any paper lying around, then that's half the card completed."

"It's all a bit of a fiddle then!"

"Not really, Haggis." he said, sparks flying from his pipe as he blew into it instead of puffing "you've got to fight fire with fire!"

"You'll be good at that!" I said, tring not to breathe in the little bits of floating ash.

He went on to explain "What I mean is, the time and motion people made up these impossible times. We use the same sort of tactics and adjust the situation to get top bonus!"

I scratched my head "You'll need to teach me all the ins and outs of this 'applied psychology'."

"If you're here long enough, you'll learn. It's an art, beating the system!"

Laughing, I said "You've certainly got it down to a fine art, the student should be with you."

Looking thoughtful, he tapped his teeth with the stem of his pipe "Yes, I think I'll get a job as a college lecturer."

"What subject would you lecture on?"

He still looked pensive "How about 'Getting the best out of time without motion!'?"

"You're a card, Tom." I said with a grin "Tony Hancock's not dead while you're alive!"

"He made more money than I ever will at this job!" he said with a sigh.

Two women turned the corner and came walking towards us.

Tom spied them, quickly laid his pipe on the cart and with a curt "Shovel, Haggis!" picked up a brush and swept some dirt along the gutter. I grabbed the shovel and held it for him to push the dirt into.

The two ladies walked past, giving us a nice smile.

"That was a bit of a fraud, Tom." I said "You're an actor as well. It's the stage you should be on."

He chuckled "Got to please the public . . ." then he let out a roar "Hell's bells!" and started dancing up and down waving his arms.

"O.K. Tom, I know you can act." I said, then following his gaze I saw the reason for his Irish jig. The contents of the cart were burning merrily. His pipe had fallen in!!

"So that's what you meant by fighting fire with fire!" I said, but Tom wasn't amused. He kept shouting "My pipe, my pipe!"

"I'll get it!" I declared and grabbed the front container where the fire was and tipped the contents onto the road. Most of stuff seemed to be combustible, papers, cartons and the like. It was now blazing fiercely!

It was my turn to dance, jumping round and round the flames trying to put them out with my feet. I must've looked like a wild redskin doing a war dance. Just at that moment a van drew up and out jumped the Bear.

"What the bloody hell are you doing, Jock?" he screamed.

I wiped my brow "I'm looking for Tom's pipe!"

"You've found the flaming thing, haven't you?" he shouted and ran back to his van. Returning with a fire extinguisher he put the flames out in a few seconds.

Tom walked over to the smouldering pile, raked about with his toe. Bending down he retrieved his old pipe and held it up. It was a little black looking but otherwise unscathed.

The Bear was raving and ranting "If you've melted that tarmac you'll both pay for the repairs to the road!"

He jumped into his van and drove off, still chunnering.

I watched him vanishing down the street, then turned to see old Tom chortling away to himself. He winked at me "You're certainly

Fire dance in Birkenhead Road, MEOLS.

making a burning impression on your first day, Haggis."

"Yeah," I said dejectedly "the Bear seems to be heated up. It's not as if we were swinging the lead."

Tom laid his pipe on the footpath to cool down "Don't worry about it. Once his blood pressure goes down and he thinks it over he'll be alright. Let's get this mess cleared up, we're a little behind time now."

We swept up the ashes and checked the tarmac. It was O.K., so we threw our gear on the cart and headed back.

Tom pushed the cart and I picked up all the flotsam and jetsam that was lying on the road and footpaths. Getting near the end of the first street a woman stopped us.

"Are you men supposed to be working?" she said in an angry voice "All you did in this street was pick up a few pieces of paper!"

"B-b-b-but . . ." I stammered.

Tom wasn't lost for words. Kindly he said to her "Could I just show you the difficulties that we street sweepers are up against?"

Her anger turned to rage "You're not in any difficulty. In fact you look as if you're out for a stroll in the country!" Catching her breath, she continued in a shrill voice "I'm a ratepayer! I pay to get the streets swept, and I demand that they are swept! I for one will be voting for privatization!"

She stepped back and waited grimly to see what effect that had on us.

I was dumbfounded, so I turned to old Tom for guidance.

He produced the card like a magician doing a card trick and held it up in front of the woman. "This is Banks Avenue we're in. Look at the card, what does it say there?" he asked her in a quiet voice while pointing to a line on the card.

She blinked, then squinted and read out loud, slowly and distinctly " 'Banks Avenue — patrol — five minutes'."

She looked from the card back to Tom "What does 'patrol' mean?"

Smiling, he replied softly but in a condescending tone "It means that we must only spend five minutes in this road. Just enough time to pick up any papers or stuff lying around. In fact the few minutes that you've been speaking to us must now come off another street!"

28

Confusion registered on her face. After a mental tussle, she said "How ridiculous! I'm extremely sorry to have held you up." With that she turned on her heel and marched off down the road.

I slapped him on the back "Good, Tom. You certainly changed her thinking!"

He gave me a pitying look "She's off our back for the time being Haggis, but I'll guarantee she hasn't changed!"

"Good grief, you heard what she said! How can you tell that she hasn't changed her attitude?"

"There's an old saying that holds true practically every time!"

"O.K., let's hear it."

Chuckling, he said "Well Haggis, it goes something like this: 'Convince a man against his will, and he will hold the same opinion still.' And I think that it applies even moreso to women."

"Tom, I think you should lecture on psychology, or is it psychiatry?"

"On this job, Haggis" he replied, kicking the wheel of the hand cart "you have to be not only a psychologist but a psychiatrist as well. I think I'll apply for the position of public relations officer."

"I hope you get it. I'll be your assistant."

Getting under way again, we made it back to the yard by five to twelve.

Tom got his lunch stuff out and said "Park the cart round the back, Haggis. We'll empty it after dinner."

As I walked into the messroom, Taffy from bin round three, said "Had a hard morning then, Haggis?"

"Not so hard," I replied "but it's been an eye opener."

"Yes," he retorted "you've got to keep your eyes open for the Bear when you're swinging the lead!"

"Not exactly what I meant." I said as I sat down for more corned beef butties.

Enjoying my lunch and listening to the chatter and banter going back and forth, I said to Tom "This crowd would make a good gang show on London Paladium."

Swallowing a mouthful of cheese, he said "I don't think so Haggis, if they cut out the swear words, half of them wouldn't know how to

29

speak, and the other half would be dumb."

"Sounds like it." I said, demolishing the last butty and closing my lunch box.

Dinner over, we emptied the cart into a large industrial bin then headed back to our territory.

We were about halfway there when a van drew past us and stopped. The Bear stepped out and came up to us.

"Tom, there's been a phone in complaint . . ." but Tom didn't let him finish. "Can't be on our round, Jim!" he said, with a pained look.

"Of course not," the Bear growled, turning his eyes upwards "it's Dovepoint Road. Nobody's been on that round for two or three weeks, you and Jock can do it before you start your other work."

Tom took off his cap and scratched his head "It'll be extra of course."

The Bear's eyebrows went up "I could cut your bonus by half for today, remember there are two of you doing one man's work."

"That's not our fault!" Tom remonstrated.

"Don't worry, both of you will be mentioned in dispatches." the bear said, lumbering off to his van.

When he was gone I turned to Tom "Will he cut our bonus?"

He stuck the pipe in his mouth unlit and chewed on the stem "No, he won't. He's got to put up a tough front, remember he has to deal with a lot of hard men."

"Yeah, I reckon that's right." I said, forgetting that we were two of the awkward ones he had to deal with.

We altered our course for Dovepoint Road. When we arrived I looked along the channels. "It looks quite clean, are we going to do it?"

He blew through his pipe then stuck it behind his ear. "Haggis, remember this and remember it well. When you're sent to a complaint, if it's bad you do it. If it's in good shape, you still do it!"

Pushing my cap back, I said "It seems unreasonable to sweep a clean street."

"You still haven't got the point! I'll elucidate!"

"Good grief Tom, watch nobody sees you!"

He looked at me in disbelief "I hope you're joking, Haggis. I thought I had in you a pedantic kindred spirit!"

"Only jesting, let's have your edifying elucidation."

He sighed "Well the object of our being here is not so much to clean the streets, but to please the residents. They pay rates and expect to see a street sweeper whether or not their street is clean or dirty."

"O.K. Tom, if that's the way of it, let's sweep up some dust."

We ran our brushes over the empty gutters of Dovepoint Road then completed our round.

The rest of the day was uneventful, so at three thirty we headed back to the yard.

We were the last of the sweepers to arrive back. Tom said "Haggis, hand in the card at the office and I'll lock up the cart and tools."

"Right" I said "and thanks for the help today."

"Think nothing of it Haggis. I'll see you in the mo ning."

I gave the card to the Bear in the office. He growled Did you do Dovepoint Road, Jock?"

"There was nothing in it." I replied cheerily.

His moustache quivered "There never is, but tha s not what I asked!"

Hurriedly I added "Tom and I swept every inch of it!"

"Good, Jock. Don't be late in the morning."

My first day was over!

Chapter 3

A DAY ON THE BINS

The alarm was set for six, but this morning I woke before the bell went off. Maybe it was because I'd now been with the council for about a month and my body was getting used to the rhythm of the working day, setting up a cycle to be followed.

My mind drifted and went back seven years to when I met my wife Jane. She'd come up from her home in Merseyside to have a week in the holiday camp at Ayr. I lived in Irvine at the time and had decided to go to the camp for a day's outing.

In the evening at the dance when we met, I felt like the north pole of a magnet meeting the south pole. Like that irreversible law of unlike poles, our mutual attraction drew us together. Her eyes were blue, her hair was soft and golden just like her nature.

. . . like a bubble bursting, the alarm bell blew my semi-conscious reminiscences into smithereens. I sat up and shook my head to waken up again. Jane opened one eye and looked at the time. "Good grief!" she moaned "Why do you keep getting up at six in the morning? You don't start work till quarter to eight!"

I retorted "It's our bread and butter! Good time keepers are appreciated, so I don't want to be late."

"Late!" she squealed "You'll be standing at the gate for an hour before they open it!"

I swung my legs over the bed "Jane honeybun," I whispered "I'm going to have some breakfast and get ready. Do you want me to make you something?"

"Buzz off! Don't make me anything," she replied yawning "I don't eat in the middle of the night!"

"It's good to have a job to go to." I said to the big lump in the bed.

"Goodbye!" came the muffled voice from under the bedclothes.

When I got to the yard the gate was closed, but I only had to wait a few minutes until the Bear arrived.

As he opened the gate he said "Bright and early again Jock, let's hope it continues."

"It will" I said adamantly "I'm a good time keeper."

He laughed. It was the first time I'd seen the Bear laugh. I didn't think it was possible.

"We'll see if you keep it up once you're on the bins." he said, reverting back to his surly manner.

I was first in the messroom, the Bear followed me in with his sheet of paper and sat down at the table.

Taffy and Andy Cap came in behind us and sat down. Taffy buried his head in the paper.

"Looks like rain." the Bear growled.

The little Welshman looked over the top of his paper "Looks bad boyo, the forecast's heavy rain all day."

"What do we do if it rains all day?" I asked the Bear.

He looked at me as if he couldn't believe what he'd heard "You bloody work! What did you think you'd do?"

"If the rain gets heavy we'll get soaked." I grumbled.

He sighed "Before you go out Jock I'll give you a chit. Take it to the stores and get a set of oilskins. You work in all weathers!"

"Thanks very much." I said, wondering whether to be pleased or not.

"Afraid you'll melt then, Haggis?" Taffy queried with a big grin on his face.

"Looks as if you've been in a few showers." I replied "You'd better not be going out today if it rains, you'll get washed down a grid!"

Taffy's grin got wider "That's why you're so tall Haggis! Big puddings don't melt in the rain, they swell till they burst!"

His remark elicited a roar of laughter from the lads in the messroom.

Licking my index finger, I chalked up an imaginary score. "One to you, Taff." I said, joining in the laughter.

The messroom gradually filled up. As more and more came in, the air got bluer and bluer with smoke, swearing and relating about their exploits with women, both real and imagined.

Skinny walked in and as he passed he said with a pseudo Scottish accent "See you, Jimmy!"

Laughing, I retorted "Yes you can, but I can't see you when you're behind your brush!"

He stopped, turned and glared at me "It's better than being a thick knuckle head like you!" he growled then sat down with a snort.

Taffy's paper was shaking as he chortled behind it. Peeking over the top, he said "You're having a losing streak today, Haggis!"

"Yeah," I said dejectedly "I think I'll go back to bed."

Dropping the paper onto his lap, he put on a pitying look and asked "Do you find it a drawback being Scotch?"

"I'm not Scotch!" I retorted vehemently.

"What are you then, a Pakistani?" he said, almost bursting his sides laughing.

Trying to keep my cool, I replied "No, I'm not a Pakistani. It's just that you can't speak English very well, Taffy. I'm a Scot, or Scottish. Scotch is whisky!"

He puckered his lips "Bloody hell, at least English is a second language to me, Haggis. You can't say that!"

Sounding the word clearly and crisply, I said "That!"

Laughing, he said "Go back to your hills, boyo. You're out of your depth amongst us civilized people down here!"

Frank, the charge hand from round one shoved the paper into his pocket "We've got a full crew, Jim."

The Bear looked up "On your way then."

Round one left the messroom with the typical clatter of experienced binmen.

Slim walked through the door still looking tired. The Bear marked his name off the list. "Your crew's complete now Sam, on your way."

Round two went out, vying with round one for a prize in the clattering stakes.

"You're still short of one, Cowboy," the Bear grunted "you can take the Beak again."

"He's not in yet." Cowboy said, tilting back his hat. "Can't we take Haggis or Skinny?"

The Bear's eyebrows began to dance "No!" he snarled "I can't let the Beak win. I'll bring him out in the van when he comes in."

Cowboy stood up. "O.K., wagons roll, boys." he bawled in his best John Wayne take off.

When they'd gone out, I turned to the inspector "How d'you know that the Beak will be in?"

He leaned back and tilted the chair. Putting on his all-knowing look, he declared "Easy, Jock. It's his little trick, he thinks we haven't cottoned on."

"What do you mean?" I asked, puzzled as to what the Beak's trick might be.

The Bear continued "He hides somewhere just outside the gate and when he sees the last bin wagon go out he'll saunter in and say 'Sorry I'm late'."

"But why?"

His left eyebrow went up, his right one went down. "Jock," he said "the Beak and money are bosom pals, but the Beak and work are mortal enemies. He wants the pay but he doesn't want to work too hard for it!"

Just at that point the Beak strolled in. "Sorry I'm late, Jim. The train left early and I just missed it."

"That's O.K.," the Bear said quietly "no problem, go on round three."

The Beak's eyes went wide. "All the bin wagons have gone out!" he squawked.

The Inspector looked straight at the reluctant sweeper and without even a blink said "Don't worry, I'll take you out in the van."

"F--- B--- C---!" cursed the Beak.

Still looking at him intently, the Bear said calmly "Go sit in the van, I'll be out in a minute."

Exit the Beak, kicking the door twice as he passed, saying "B---!"

The Bear handed me a card "Round five, day six. On your way Jock."

"Thanks." I said, and as I was taking the card, he had an afterthought. "By the way, all the litter bins on the lamp posts are full, empty them on your way up."

"O.K." I said, and went out the door, looking at the marks on it, testifying to the Beak's violent temper. He was sitting sulking in the inspector's van as I passed on my way to the stores.

I collected the oilskins, put a brush and shovel on the cart and got under way. The designated streets on the card were near the bowling green, so I headed there first.

As I pushed the cart along, I thought about the Beak. To me, he seemed to be a drop-out, a rebel against everything! Still in his teens, he was the typical product of a broken home. His father had gone off with another woman, leaving his mother to bring up four kids. A succession of step-fathers who'd illtreated the children didn't help any in his formative years. I couldn't help wondering how I would've fared if I'd been brought up in such an environment.

"Ouch! — You silly fool!!"

The yell brought me back to the scene around me. I hadn't noticed that my brush was protruding out about a yard from the cart and it had whacked a lady across her bottom. She was rubbing her posterior and yelling at me.

"I'm terribly sorry," I said, getting flummoxed "Is there anything I can do? Is it bruised?"

As I moved towards her she stepped back "Gerroff! You sex maniac, you've done enough damage!" With that she stomped off down the street.

Trying to cover my embarrassment, I hurried away leaving a little knot of people smirking on the footpath.

By the time I reached the bowling green it was nine o'clock so I went straight into the hut for my tea-break.

I was on my second butty and had drunk about half a cup of tea when the door opened and in walked the Bear.

He stood with arms akimbo "Caught again Jock!" he proclaimed in a sharp authoritative tone.

"B-ut, b-ut. . ." I spluttered through a mouthful of corned beef and brown bread.

With a sigh he said "Don't overtax your brains trying to think of excuses. Jump in the van and I'll take you to round three."

Packing up my remaining butties and quickly swigging the half cup of tea, I asked "Has the Beak gone sick?"

"No, Taffy's been bitten by a dog. He's gone to hospital for an anti-tet jab, then he's going home."

"Poor dog," I said consolingly "is it alright? Do you think it'll survive?"

He rolled his eyes upwards "Bloody hell, why do I get all the comedians? Come on, hide your cart round the back and get in the van."

The Bear was in the van before me and I'd hardly touched leather when we shot off with a screech!

"Ever been to Silverstone, Jim?" I asked with a grin.

Taking his eyes off the road, he turned his head and glared at me. "I hope you're not being sarky!" he snarled.

"No — no!" I asserted "By the way, where are round three working, Jim?"

"They're in Greasby." he answered curtly, blowing his horn at a dog running loose on the road. "Bloody thing!" he added.

I plunged in at the deep end "You can usually tell peoples' character by the way they treat animals."

Again the glare "Jock, there are no bad dogs! Only bad dog owners. That one shouldn't be on the loose!"

That finished the conversation about dogs!

Trying to sweeten the atmosphere, I said "Is Greasby a good area?"

"Bins are bins wherever they are." he replied drily.

When we got to Greasby, we found a street with empty bins lined up each side but not a binman in sight.

"Where are they all?" I asked in amazement.

"What were you doing when I found you?" the Bear growled.

"That's good" I replied "maybe I can finish my tea-break now."

He snorted "Let's hope you sweat all that tea out of you instead of looking for toilets all day!"

When we found them, right enough there they were all in the cab supping tea.

We both got out and the Bear said "Here's your replacement, Cowboy. Make him work hard, see what all that haggis and whisky has done for him!"

"Thanks, Jim." the Cowboy said, then to me "How many spoons Haggis?"

"Two." I replied and grabbed the steaming mug he handed down to me.

The Bear drove off in his van chunnering about tea Jennys.

I hadn't quite finished my tea when Andy Cap and a fellow nicknamed Jim Lad jumped out the wagon and disappeared up the street.

Nodding in their direction, I asked the Cowboy "Where are they going?"

"They're trucking," he replied "they pull out the full bins ahead of us."

I handed the empty mug back up to the Cowboy, then gazed at the mess round the wagon. The ground round about was a right mess, littered with crusts of bread, wrappings and tea slops that had been thrown out the window of the wagon.

Cowboy, Billy and the Beak jumped out the cab. "Haggis," Cowboy said "I'm tipping with the Beak, you and Billy take the empties back, he'll show you what to do."

I fell into step beside Billy and we walked back along the street to where the empty bins started.

"Been on the bins long?" I asked him.

"Five years, give or take."

"Do you like it?"

He screwed up his nose "Not really, but it brings in the ackers."

When we reached the first of the empties, he pointed across the street "You take that side Haggis, I'll do t'other."

Lifting the first bin, I walked up the path. As I put it down a lady came out the house. She looked in the bin then at me. "You've left half the rubbish in the bin!" she said angrily.

My hackles began to rise. "That" I said, giving the bin a tap with my toe "is the first bin I've lifted!"

"That's no excuse. Look at the stuff you've left in it!" she squealed.

"Lady, it's not me, it's the ones who tip!"

Wagging her finger at me, her squeal rose an octave "You're soliciting gratuities! I'm going to report you!"

"Don't you know what tipping means?" I protested.

She was now hopping from one foot to the other. "Get out! You're getting nothing!"

Turning on my heel, I muttered "Stupid old bat!"

38

"What did you say?" she screamed.

I shouted over my shoulder "Behind your bin, it's an old cat!"

Going out the gate, I could hear her calling "Tiddles, here Tiddles."

Billy was now well in front, so I broke into a jog-trot as I took the empties back along the one side of the street. Even going flat out it took me about an hour before I caught up with him. At the last house in that street I took the bin up the drive, put it down, replaced the lid and turned to leave.

"You!" a woman's voice screamed behind me.

"Are you speaking to me?" I asked the hatchet faced female that had appeared.

"Yes, who do you think I'm speaking to? I want my dustbin returned to it's proper place!"

"Where would that be — the Apache reservation?" I inquired sarcastically as I mopped sweat from my brow.

"You insolent man! It belongs here!" she retorted haughtily, indicating a spot two yards from where I'd placed it. I slid it across with my foot and walked away.

"I'm going to report you!" she shouted after me down the path "We'll get better service when you're private!"

By the time we'd worked for about another hour I was wet with perspiration. Billy appeared out of a gate on the other side of the street.

"Flaming hard work this, isn't it?" I expostulated.

"You kidding?" he replied, and I couldn't even see a bead of sweat on him "This is the easy part! Wait till you start tipping or trucking!"

In about another twenty minutes the wagon appeared. Billy shouted across "Leave the rest Haggis, jump in the wagon, we go back for dinner break now."

I scrambled into the cab over old batteries, scrap metal and all sorts of bric-a-brac. There must've been as much junk in the cab as there was in the back of the wagon. Squeezing in between Andy Cap and Billy, I sat down hard on an old statuette that Cowboy had rescued. "Ouch! — Flaming junk!" I cried out, pulling the offending object out from under my rump. Cowboy leaned over and grabbed it from me. Forgetting the John Wayne drawl, he reverted to his native Scouse "I'll marmalise yer, Haggis. This ain't slummy, it's for me mantlepiece!"

39

Billy laughed "You can hardly get in his house, Haggis. Cowboy's our champion rooter."

Andy Capp chipped in "Yeah, he's the original rootin-tootin Cowboy."

The Cowboy responded by laying down his figurine, then with a flourish took off his hat and proceeded to beat Andy Cap over the head with it.

When we got to the messroom I was glad to sit down on a chair. Jim Lad made the tea in a big black pot for the gang. Black wasn't the original colour. It looked as if it might be made of aluminium, but you couldn't tell. 'Well' I thought 'It won't matter if he forgets to put in the dry tea, it'll still be a strong brew!'

Dinner over, we all climbed into the wagon again and headed for Greasby.

As we rattled along, the Beak moaned to Cowboy "I hurt my arm this morning, it's very sore."

Cowboy scowled "You're a permanent pain. You can take back thisavvy, Haggis can come tipping w'me."

That brought a smirk to the Beak's face.

When we reached the first of the empties, Billy and the Beak jumped out. The driver carried on till we reached the full bins. We all baled out then, Andy Cap and Jim Lad going ahead.

Cowboy pushed his hat back a little "O.K. Haggis, now we'll test your mettle. You take one side, I'll take t'other, any very heavy ones we'll double up."

After about an hour tipping, I came to the conclusion that what I'd done this morning, carrying back the empties was like sitting in an office compared with this. Now I realised why that little smirk had appeared on the Beak's face.

We were working along another street when a shapely young girl walked past.

"There's a nice pair of pins, Cowboy!" I said, leering at the curvatious hunk of femininity.

His eyes went wide and he bellowed "Wa-hoo!" Then resting the full bin on the edge of the wagon he gave a long low wolf whistle. That was followed by a bang, then a loud metalic grinding noise as the bin was smashed by one of the arms of the crusher!

Cowboy gawped at the wagon chewing up the bin. "Bloody hell Haggis, now look what you've done!"

"Me?" I croaked, standing back and watching in amazement as the crushed bin slowly vanished into the bowels of the wagon.

"What do we do about that?" I asked with a gulp, starting to get panicky.

"Nothing, Haggis." he replied quite cheerily, then roared "Hi-e-up" to the driver. The bin wagon lurched forward to the next set of bins.

After we'd worked another two streets I was just getting over the crushed bin episode when I took the lid off a large metal bin. It was filled to the brim with old paint tins. Straight into the well of the wagon I tipped the lot.

"Haggis! Duck!" Cowboy roared at my back.

"Yer what'?" I asked naïvely, but it was too late! The force of the crusher arms had burst one of the tins, the contents of which sprayed up and outward; splattering paint down the side of my face and jacket.

The Cowboy was chortling "Nice shade of red, Haggis!"

Wiping off as much as I could with an old rag, we carried on tipping.

We managed another three streets before the next traumatic occurrence. With a groan and a couple of clanks the crusher gave up the ghost.

Laying his full bin down on the road with a crash, Cowboy spat into the rubbish in the well. "Bloody pig!" he cursed, scratching his head.

"That's us finished for the day?" I asked, sighing with relief at getting a break.

"Bloody hell, no!" he replied irritably, "We've eight more streets to do. Andy Cap and Jim Lad'll have all the full bins pulled out. If we finish now we'll have to put 'em all back."

"What's the score then?" I asked, resting my weary bones as I sat on the next bin to be tipped.

After another good scratch at his head he came up with the answer.

"It's too near stopping time to call out the mechanics." he said with a frown "You'll need to get up and kick the muck into the well with your feet!"

I stood back aghast "Me? — Why me?" I asked, horrified.

"You're the new boy, Haggis. Up you go!" he chuckled, giving me a punt up onto the edge of the well.

It wasn't too bad with only Cowboy tipping, but after five minutes Andy Cap and Jim Lad came back, having pulled out the daily quota of bins.

With the three of them tipping I was hard pushed to kick the rubbish in. The pace was fast and furious! I was almost at collapsing point when a lady came running up shouting and waving her arms "My purse! My purse! The kid's thrown my purse in the bin!"

The three tippers turned and gazed at the apparition while I sank back into the rubbish with a grateful sigh

Feet pattering, the lady rushed up to the wagon, completely ignoring the three binnies. She leaned over the edge and looked into the well. She didn't find her purse, but what she did see was me lying all out between the teeth of the crusher, red paint the colour of blood spattered over my face and clothes.

If I live to be a hundred I don't think I'll ever hear a scream like that again. It was piercing, reaching a crescendo then fading to nothing as she collapsed in a dead faint.

The three of them looked down at the poor woman, perplexity written on their faces.

"Bloody hell Haggis, now look what you've done!" Cowboy groaned.

Kneeling in the well, I stuck my head over the edge and peered down at the woman lying on her back, face white as chalk. Her eyelids flickered and with a little moan opened them wide. Again it was unfortunate that the first thing she saw was my red-streaked, sweaty face gazing at her from above.

If banshees were real, I'm sure they'd be envious of the wail that this lady produced before she swooned into oblivion again.

A few neighbours had come out to see what was going on. The poor lady was carried back to her house while Cowboy, Billy and I rooted in the rubbish for her purse. Cowboy found it and held it up in triumph.

Billy winked at me "Told you he's our champion rooter!"

Cowboy ignored him and walked back to the lady's house to return the purse. He was in there for about ten minutes, verifying that

Fainting lady in Rigby Drive, GREASBY.

she was alright and explaining the situation.

By this time all the men were back so it didn't take long to get the rest of the bins on. When all the empties had been returned everybody jumped into the cab. All that is except me. I dragged myself in with great difficulty.

When we got back to the yard I stepped out, staggering as I landed on the ground.

Billy jumped down after me like a gazelle "Don't worry too much Haggis" he laughed "a few weeks tipping and you'll be in tip-top shape."

Cowboy looked as fit as a fiddle "C'mon Haggis, we're going for a bevvy. I'll mug yer to a jar if y'like."

"No thanks" I replied wearily "I'm going to sit down for a few minutes. I might come up later."

"Right y'ar." he said with a laugh and walked off.

Once I'd recovered sufficiently I went up to the Ship Inn. When I went in Cowboy was standing at the bar, his glass almost empty. I ordered a pint of bitter.

"How do you feel after your first day, Haggis?" he asked, smiling benignly.

"A bit sore." I replied, sinking about half my pint in one easy movement.

"So am I," he said, brow furrowing "but it's not the bins that caused it!"

"What was it then?"

"I caught a dose when I was in the Middle East." he said without even blinking.

"You shouldn't go with bad women!" I said, feeling righteous "It's your own fault."

"It's nothing like that." he laughed "It's a common disease out there, it's called 'Yurs'."

"What's 'Yurs'?" I asked innocently.

"Thanks very much Haggis. " he grinned "I'll have a pint of bitter."

"Good Gordon Highlanders!" I groaned, paying for his drink.

"Thanks Haggis." he said, supping his fresh pint with gusto.

"How many does he catch with that?" I asked the barman.

"Only the new ones." he replied "I thought he'd played it out by now."

Cowboy glanced over his shoulder, then winked at me "Here comes the student, catch him with that gag."

The student came up to the bar. "You're on sand John, you'll get caught coming in here at this time!" I told him.

"It's my tea-break." he replied. "You look a bit weary, Haggis are you alright?"

'This is going to be easy.' I thought. "No," I said "it's my old trouble coming back. I caught it out East, it's called 'Yurs'."

The student looked pensive "I've read about that, but it's not yurs, it's Y.A.R.S." he said, spelling it out. "It's pronounced yars."

"What is yars?" I asked, as gullible as ever.

"A pint of lager! Thanks Haggis."

"A hundred Good Gordon Highlanders! I'm too tired." I said paying for his drink and walking out.

They were all roaring with laughter as I left.

My first day on the bins was finished and I felt the same!

Chapter 4

BACK ON THE BRUSH

Jane was going to her mother's for the week-end on her own. "You're no use to me in this state!" she grumbled as she put on her overcoat. "I hope this job isn't going to knock the stuffing out of you!"

Struggling to keep my eyes open, I retorted "A few weeks on the bins and I'll be the fittest man around!"

"If it doesn't kill you first!" she muttered, glaring at me sprawled in the chair.

"I'll be alright if you're here to make decent meals for me, and while we're at it don't put red leather on my butties again!"

Tilting her nose, she said "Huh!" and flounced out.

Getting some cans of ale in, I kept to the house and had a good rest for two days.

When she returned on Sunday night her attitude had changed. Ignoring the state I'd got the house into, she flung her arms round my neck, kissed me and said "Hello darling, it's good to be back. I did miss you!"

"What's wrong? Did you and your mother have an argument?"

"Don't be like that Steve, don't let's fight. You know the old saying?"

I sighed "No, tell me."

Her eyes glistened "It's 'Make love, not war.' let's have a little drink and go to bed." she purred, giving me a warm wet kiss.

She didn't need to force me too much. Filling her glass with gin and tonic, I chose a straight whiskey. As I took them into the bedroom, I thought 'I hope I'm not on the bins tomorrow'. . .

When I got to the yard in the morning, the messroom was already half-full. Amazingly, the general conversation wasn't about the varied sexual exploits but the coming change-over from council control of cleansing to private ownership.

"Writing's on the wall for you, Haggis." Taffy piped up "Last in — first out! That's the rule!"

Laughing, I said "No problem, I'll go sign-writing!"

Eyebrows going up, he looked over his paper at me with a quizzical expression "Sign-writing?" he questioned.

"Yes," I chortled "I'll just go down to the dole office and sign my name by writing it on the dotted line!"

Giving a loud raspberry, he groaned "Bloody hell Haggis, you're getting worse."

Old Tom spoke up "Jim, the prom's in a terrible mess, all the litter bins and baskets are chock-a-block. There's litter everywhere!"

The Bear's eyebrows always did a slow foxtrot when he was thinking. At last they stopped and his moustache took over "Take Jock with you," he said "and both of you do the prom this morning. In the afternoon you can help him with his round. That way you won't lose any bonus."

"O.K.," Tom said "that sounds a good idea."

The tempo of the Bear's eyebrows changed quickly to 4-4 time, and a hairy tango didn't augur anything good.

"Jock, you and Tom come into the yard for your tea-break at quarter past nine!"

"What if we're up the other end?" I asked, knowing of course that he must have a reason; one that I knew I wasn't going to like.

He scowled at me "The manager wants you in his office at nine thirty sharp!"

The buzz of conversation died as everyone took to listening, waiting for the whys and wherefores of the Bear's latest remark.

Trying to act surprised and innocent, I asked "Why, what's wrong?"

Pursing his lips, he replied "You were reported twice on Friday!"

Feigning bewilderment, I croaked "What for?"

"You should know, Jock!" he growled "Once for insolence and once for soliciting gratuities!"

"That's not true," I pleaded "at least about the gratuities anyway."

Spreading his hands, he said "Don't try to convince me." Then pointing with his thumb towards the office, continued "Convince the manager at nine thirty!"

Once everyone knew the score, the hum of voices started up again. What anyone was saying, I didn't know as I was too busy thinking of how to answer the charges.

We got out the yard before eight o'clock. Tom and I took a cart each and some plastic bags.

Getting into step beside me, Tom grinned "Make sure you've got your gloves Haggis, you'll need them in dog-alley!"

I looked at him ambling along with a big grin on his face "What'you on about, I thought we were to do the prom?"

We stopped while he lit his pipe. Between puffs he said "That's right, Hoylake promenade — alias — dog-alley! you'll find out!"

We started at the south end of the prom. At the first bin we stopped, Tom drew on his gloves and I followed suit.

He said "We have to empty these small ones by hand, never put your hand in a bin without your glove on!"

When we reached the fourth bin I found out why. Putting my hand in the bin and grabbing the muck, I pulled it out. The brown stuff was oozing through my fingers.

"Good Gordon Highlanders! What's that!" I squawked, holding it well away from me and knowing by the pong what it really was.

He laughed "Don't you recognise dog shit when you see it?"

"Yu-uck, what'll I do with it?" I wailed, thinking as I said it what a stupid question it was.

"Drop it and your glove into the cart. I've got a spare pair, and the Bear'll give you new ones when we get back."

Looking in amazement at the height of the bin from the ground, I said "It must've been a Great Dane!"

"No, not even a Great Dane, Haggis. It was a pig!"

"A pig?"

"Yes, a human pig!"

"Tom," I said "pigs are clean animals or so I've heard."

As we moved along to the next bin, Tom explained "Haggis, the people who do this think they are clean. They're incensed at all the dog shit on the prom. Thinking that the cleansing department don't do enough, they come with litle shovels and scoop it into the bins."

"But what about us?" I said, grueing at the thought of it sticking to my fingers "We'll get beriberi or something!"

He chuckled "Remember what the Bear said, we're the dregs of humanity. Come on let's go, it'll give you an appetite for your corned beef butties."

"Now I know why you smoke a pipe. One pong kills t'other!" I retorted, as I watched him puffing contentedly.

When we'd gone a bit further, I put my hand into another bin and pulled out a package. It was neatly wrapped and tied with string. Holding it up, I said "Look here Tom, someone's lost a parcel."

Taking the pipe from his mouth he peered at the package, then screwed up his face. "Back there you got filth on your hand, if you open that you'll get filth for your mind!"

Sometimes I couldn't tell when he was joking. "Come off it Tom. You can't tell what's in here."

"I can, you know." he said, pointing to the parcel with his smouldering pipe "It's porn books. Someone doesn't want his wife or mother to see them so he tosses them in here."

I didn't believe him so I opened the parcel. Just as he'd said, it was porn books. Hard porn at that. I leafed through a couple of the glossy magazines. The pictures would make your hair stand on end.

Tom was sitting on the cart, puffing on his old pipe and watching me intently. I closed the magazines and held them out. "You want these, Tom?"

"No," he said, blowing out a cloud of smoke "I've no use for that kind of stuff."

"I don't want them either." I said, tossing the lot into the cart "I don't need anything like that, I've got enough to contend with at home with Jane. She thinks I'm Tarzan."

"You're lucky." he said, smiling wanly "That the wife?"

"Yeah, that's right." I replied "Did you ever marry, Tom?"

"The wife died ten years ago." he said in a low sad voice, and his eyes were just as sad as the memories came flooding back.

I could feel his grief "Sorry about that," was all I could think of to say "didn't you ever consider it again?"

He smiled wryly "No, I've had my day, just like every dog!"

49

Trying desperately to lift his spirits, I decided to tack "Yeah, and I bet you've been a gay old dog in your time!"

It worked, his face broke into a grin. Knocking out his pipe, he said "We'll be for it if we don't get moving, Haggis."

We got back to the yard by ten past nine. I was just about to enjoy my last butty when the Bear walked into the messroom "Mister Howard is waiting for you in the office, Jock." he announced in a dictatorial voice.

I smiled up at him "O.K., I'm just finishing my tea."

"*Now!*" he roared, eyebrows threatening to tango. I leaped to my feet and followed him into the office.

"Good morning Mister Mackenzie, please take a seat." said the manager, sitting behind a desk which seemed very much smaller than the Inspector's.

"Good morning, sir." I responded, standing there like a big wet leek.

"Sit down, Jock." the Bear said irritably, bringing a chair round to the front of the desk.

I sat facing Mister Howard. The Bear stood by the manager's left.

The manager started the ball rolling. Leaning back in the chair and folding his arms, he said "Mister Mackenzie, on Friday we had two complaints about a binman from round three. The description and the accent fits you perfectly. We'll deal with them one at a time. Firstly, did you solicit gratuities?"

Trying my best to put on a grieved expression, I declared "Certainly not!"

He leaned forward and put his hands on the desk "Well, a lady said that you did. Was there anything you can remember saying that would make her think that?"

Taking a little time to reply, I said slowly "Ye-e-es, it must've been the first bin that I took back. . ."

"Go on." the manager prompted.

"Well," I continued "the lady complained that it hadn't been emptied properly. I told her it wasn't my fault, it was the ones who tip."

"Ah" the manager said, leaning back again "she must've thought that you wanted a tip to empty it properly."

I nodded "That's what I imagine."

He looked up at the Bear "What do you think?"

The inspector looked at me narrowly as he stroked his chin "It seems pretty likely." he said "I'd let that one go."

Mister Howard turned back to face me again "Alright, we'll forget about that one. The other complaint was, that you called a lady an Apache Indian!"

"It wasn't quite like that!" I remonstrated.

Elbows on the desk, he rested his chin on his hands as if it was going to take a long time "Alright," he said "explain."

"Well," I said "when I returned the bin, it seemed that I didn't put it where she wanted it. She had a place reserved for it that was a bit patchy, so I said to her 'That looks like a patchy reservation!'"

The manager laughed "Hell's bells, couldn't you think up a better one than that?"

"No," I said dejectedly "that's the best I could do in the time. If I'd known on Friday that I'd be on the carpet, I could've drummed up something better over the weekend."

"Alright," he said, laying the palms of his hands flat on the desk and trying to look stern "it's obvious you were insolent to that lady. You'll lose half a day's bonus for Friday, also take a severe warning. We must have good public relations. I know it's difficult at times, but you must be pleasant to the public."

"Alright, I'll try." I said with a grin.

"You can go now." he said, glancing at the Bear and trying to hide a smile.

Tom was waiting for me "How'd it go Haggis, did you get a bollocking?"

"Wasn't too bad," I chuckled "docked half a day's bonus and a strong warning."

He knocked out his pipe "Could've been worse," he said "but you'll need to watch how you talk to the public. Some are quick to phone in, but having said that, I can tell you, most of the public are sympathetic. In fact, on Friday a lady gave me a tip."

"Just like me to miss that," I grumbled "how much?"

"A nicker."

I whistled "Not bad, if you got a few like that every week it would help."

He moued his lips "Not so many at this time of year, but when Christmas comes we get a fair amount. That shows that most of the public appreciate binmen and sweepers."

"O.K.," I said, glancing back at the office "let's go before the Bear comes out and hauls me back onto the carpet for loitering."

As we sauntered back to the prom I said to Tom "It's fairly obvious to me that you haven't always been a sweeper. What did you do before you started with the council?"

He didn't alter his step or turn his head "Do you really want to know?"

"Yeah, sure. That's why I asked!"

A short silence then he said "I was a teacher."

"Good Gordon Highlanders! A teacher! What did you teach?" I queried.

"Science. he said matter-of-factly.

I was taken aback "Good grief, from teaching science to shovelling muck! Why?"

"Haggis, I just didn't like it!" he said emphatically "Shut in all day, coping with kids. I wanted to be out in the open air, with a job that didn't entail a lot of concentration and worry. Hey presto, along came this job. Who else but the council would pay you to stroll along the prom every day?"

Chuckling, I replied "I tend to agree with you. It's half the battle if you enjoy your work."

"Yes, I enjoy it Haggis, and I don't get ulcers worrying. What about you? What's your murky past?"

Sighing as I thought back, I told him "I used to be a moto. mechanic, but hated every minute of it. Stuck under cars, covered in black oil. It wasn't my cup of tea!"

With a twinkle in his eye he said "Yes, you're better here, it's good clean, filthy muck you get on this job."

We both had a good laugh, then we buckled in to get our work completed. We finished off the prom in double quick time and headed back to the yard for dinner break.

Lunch over, I picked up a sweeper's card at the office. It was round five, day one. Tom and I took one cart this time. We threw on two brushes and two shovels then headed for the round.

There wasn't a cloud in the sky. The fact that there was no wind made the sun seem that much hotter. I began to sweat just pushing the cart. First, off came my jacket. Next I shed my cardigan.

"Aren't you taking anything off, Tom?" I asked him, looking at all the clothes he was wearing.

"If it gets any warmer, I might." he said without even a trace of a smile.

It was a warm, sticky and dusty afternoon, but finally we completed our round and wearily wended our way back.

When we arrived at the yard and had emptied the cart, Tom said "You take the card back to the office and I'll put the tools away."

The inspector was waiting by the office door "Your round completed, Jock?" he asked as I handed him the card.

"Yes, everything's O.K."

"Close your eyes!" he barked.

I turned round to see if there was anyone else there that he could possibly be speaking to. We were the only two in the vicinity.

"Pardon?" I said, thinking I'd heard wrongly.

"Are you deaf? Close your eyes!" he bellowed.

Thinking that it was a joke, I said "Are you going to give me something?"

His eyebrows were getting ready for a samba! "Jock," he spat out "go on the stage if you want to be a comedian! Close your eyes!"

I closed my eyes smartly and waited in anticipation.

"Open up." he said almost immediately.

Completely mystified, I asked querulously "What was that in aid of?"

"It's for your bonus, Jock. Don't be late in the morning."

Head swimming, I went out to the sweepers' shed. Old Tom had just finished putting the gear away.

"Hey," I said "I think the Bear's going bonkers!"

53

Locking the shed door, he turned round with a smile "Why, what's up Jock? Was it the old eye trick?"

Surprised, I said "That's right, the mind boggles. What's it all about?"

"Well Haggis, it's been a really hot sunny day, hasn't it?"

"Tom," I replied "I'm a bit slow. It's been hot, so what?"

"Think about it." he said, pointing to his eyes "If you worked all day with your eyes open, your lids would be white, but if you'd found a quiet corner to lie down and sun bathe with your eyes closed, they'd be brown. The Bear's not daft. If your lids had've been brown, he'd mark you down for a low bonus, because he'd know you'd been skiving! D'you get the picture?"

"Good Gordon Highlanders! I think I'll go to night school to study psychology!" I said, scratching my head.

He laughed, "You'll learn more here, Haggis, just give it a few months."

"O.K. Tom, I'll see you in the morning." I said, heading for home instead of going to the pub.

When I arrived at the house, Jane was waiting for me. As soon as I opened the door she started jumping up and down, waving an envelope.

"You've got a letter! You've got a letter!" she squealed.

"Looks like you've read it." I said, taking off my jacket and sinking into a chair.

She knelt on the floor beside my chair and took the letter out of the envelope "It's from the Post Office," she said as she handed it to me "they're offering you a job."

I looked at the letter, then at Jane "I applied for this job five months ago!"

Raising her voice, she cried out "So what, they want you now!"

"They didn't want me then!" I retorted "The council gave me a job when I needed one."

She got up and stood, legs apart, arms akimbo "What are you trying to say?"

"I want to be loyal to those who gave me a job when we were desperate." I said firmly.

54

She was aghast. Her mouth dropped open, then managed to blurt out "But they're making you redundant soon!"

My face was set "Doesn't matter. I'm staying put! I'll face that when it comes."

Eyes blazing, she pointed her finger at me "You're stupid, you are!" she roared, then stomped out.

'Her mother's going to get an earful' I thought as I went to the kitchen to get something to eat.

Chapter 5

SAND IN MY SANDWICHES

By now I was well seasoned to the job. Most of the time I'd spent on the brush, but quite a number of odd days I'd gone on the bin wagon, replacing men who were off sick.

On this particular day in July when I arrived at the yard, the Bear was already in the messroom, paper and pen in front of him, waiting to tick off the names as everyone appeared.

He glanced up as I came in "Going to be hot today again, Jock."

"Certainly is." I said, looking at him sitting there with a big heavy tweed jacket on.

"Big wind last night!" he continued, determined to keep the conversation going.

I responded "Never heard it, I'm a heavy sleeper. Anything blown down?"

One eyebrow went up, the other went down as he replied "No, up!"

I tried hard to digest that remark but couldn't, so I had to ask him "How up?"

"Sand, Jock. Sand!" he grated "Tons of it, blown up from the beach onto the prom, about a two or three hundred yard stretch of it!"

I laughed "You've got a problem there, Jim."

His eyebrows were taking partners for a foxtrot "Not me! I've no problem, but you lot have! You'll be putting it all back where it belongs!"

The messroom began to fill up. The Beak came in and quietly sat down in a corner.

'Unusual for him' I thought 'he must be mulling over some plan how to avoid working too hard.'

Old Tom came in and started speaking before the door had closed behind him "Have you seen all the sand on the prom, Jim?"

"Could anybody miss it?" the Bear growled, his eyes rolling upwards.

The Beak sidled over to where the inspector was sitting. He put his hands on the desk and leaned over. "I'd like to go on the bins today, Jim" he said very quietly.

The Bear seemed bemused. It was the first time I'd seen his eyebrows do a cha—cha. Recovering quickly, he hammered on the table with his hands "Attention everybody." he roared, then to the Beak "Say that again."

The unusual request was repeated "I'd like to go on the bins! What's wrong with that?" he declared, looking daggers at everybody.

A deafening cheer broke out in the messroom, some clapping, others stamping their feet. When the hubbub died down, the Bear leaned forward, glared at the Beak and snarled "Request denied, you're on sand today!"

"F--- b--- c---!" the Beak bawled and turned to go.

The Bear growled "Didn't know you could speak French, did you go to night school?"

"You're a bloody French word!" the Beak spluttered, livid with rage.

The Bear's eyebrows were doing a jig. Two new dances in one day! This was really something. His eyes though were steady, boring into the sullen sweeper "You're now on very dangerous ground, watch it or you'll be sorry!"

The Beak snorted and walked out the door, kicking it as he passed, muttering profanities under his breath.

The bin rounds were gradually filling up and left as soon as they got their full crews. Round two went first, then round one. Three was last as usual, waiting for one man.

The last of round three came in, it was a guy nicknamed Rooster. The Bear checked him off the list and motioned to the charge hand "O.K. Cowboy, you're crewed up. On your way."

They all clattered out. The noisiest crew of all!

Turning to Tom, I asked "How did Rooster get a monica like that?"

He took a long drag at his pipe then blew out a cloud of smoke "Goes back to his school days, Haggis. One day in French class the teacher called him out. 'Translate these verbs on the blackboard!' he told him. Poor Phil couldn't remember any, so the teacher said 'Go back to your roost, boy!' He's been saddled with the name Rooster ever since."

"Doesn't he mind?"

"No, slides off, like water off a duck's back."

Surveying the remnants left in the messroom, the Bear said "Tom, you tidy Market Street then go on sand. Jock, Skinny and Beak, you lot take a barrow each and some brushes and shovels. Go down to the prom and shift the sand back onto the beach. I'll follow you down in the van shortly and detail a section each. That way I'll know who's been working."

We all trooped out happy as sandboys, except for the Beak, that is. He was waiting just outside, sullen as Satan.

Getting our gear from the shed, we started for the prom. It must've been a funny sight. Tom leading the convoy, with his little green cart, then three sweepers with wheelbarrows in line behind him. We drew more than a few peculiar glances as we sauntered through the streets like loonies. Tom turned off and headed for Market Street, while we followed the smell of the ozone and made for the seashore.

When we got to the prom we all sat down, determined not to do anything before the Bear arrived. We were afraid we might do the wrong bit and he would assign us to another piece of the prom.

We'd only been sitting for a few minutes when the Bear drove up. He jumped out the van and came over, face like thunder. "I see you're all in your favourite positions, sitting on your backsides!"

The Beak looked up and squinted, shielding his eyes against the morning sun. "Waiting for instructions." he said but not making any effort to get up.

The Bear glared at us, a hairy tango starting on his face. "If any of you can stand up I'll show you the sections I want done."

We all got to our feet, the Beak needing a little help. Once he showed us what he required, the inspector said "I'll be checking again at dinner time." with that he roared off in his van — the Beak sat down again!

Moving up to my delegated section, I attacked the drifted piles of sand with gusto.

It was demoralising work. The sand was dry and fine, tending to run off the shovel as soon as I loaded it. By the time I'd cleared about five yards, Old Tom appeared.

"You haven't done Market Street already, have you?" I asked him in surprise.

"Yeah, wind's blown everything away, just emptied the litter bins." then looking around, added "Where's the other two?"

"Don't know, they vanished ten minutes ago. Maybe they've gone on a lemming march." I said pointing to the sea.

He laughed "No such luck, they'll have gone to the station kiosk for tea-break."

Dropping my shovel, I sat on the sand with my back against the wall, looking across the prom to the sea. "I'm having mine right now. My belly thinks my throat's cut!"

"Mine too." he said and sank down beside me.

Opening up my butties, I bit into a nice corned beef one made with brown bread — it was full of sand!

"Good grief" I spluttered, spitting it all out "now I know why they're called sandwiches!"

"Actually Haggis, they got their name from a Lord, Lord Sandwich." Tom assured me.

"You could've fooled me, this seems a better explanation. Never mind, I'm going to eat them, sand or no sand!"

Tom opened up one of his butties, looked at it and laughed "I've got cheese on mine again. Good stuff this cheese, it keeps you going."

"Oh," I chortled "I thought it was the other way, doesn't it bind you up?"

He ignored that and asserted "Full of protein, Haggis. Gives you strength."

"Don't you ever get lonely, Tom, living on your own? Nobody to have your meals ready for you or make up your butties?"

"Not really," he replied as he chomped his cheese "some nights I go down to the pub and have a game of darts. When I get home I watch telly. During the day I've the public to talk to. Never have time to be lonely!"

"Yeah, you seem happy enough, that's good."

Just then a well dressed lady came along with a dog on a lead. It stopped abruptly, pulling it's owner to a halt. It shit in front of us . . .

Tom's butty stopped halfway to his mouth, his eyes glued to the dog. The lady stood and smiled at her little pet. When it had finished, she gushed "That's a good boy, come along now." then made to walk off.

Tom jumped to his feet and rushed over "Hold on a minute, lady," he said "don't you know that it's an offence to let a dog foul the footpath?"

She cocked her snoot in the air "Don't be impertinent, I'll report you when I get back!" she said haughtily, peering at Tom through her glasses.

"Madam," he retorted "if I report you when I get back, you could go to court and be fined heavily! You've just broken the law. In fact a lot of people hate dogs because of owners who don't think."

"I've got to take Rinty out." she wailed, almost in tears "What can I do?"

"It's simple," Tom replied in a quiet sympathetic voice "when the dog stops, pull him over to the channel and let him do his needs in there."

She smiled "Alright my man, thank you for your advice, I'll try that in future." then pointing to the heapo on the footpath, said "Ah-hem, what shall I do about that?"

Tom gave a sniff "We'll remove it for you this time, but it just needs a little thought by dog owners, it would save a lot of agro."

"Thanks." she said, and walked off.

He came back over again and sat down with a grunt.

"I liked the way you handled that, Tom." I said, giving him the thumbs up. "If I'd gone over, I would've given her the big stick and got myself into trouble."

"The calm approach is always best, Haggis." he declared as he beat hell out of his butties in an effort to remove the sand.

"Do you like dogs?" I asked him as he made heavy weather of his gritty red leather sarnie.

"Can take 'em or leave 'em," he replied as he spat out a half chewed mouthful "but we'd better get mobile or we'll be in the doghouse if the Bear catches us chewing the stinking sand instead of shovelling it!"

Tom put some sand on the heapo, scooped it up on his shovel and dropped it into the gulley. We then resumed our task of barrowing the sand back onto the beach.

It took the four of us two days to move the sand back, but finally we made it. The Bear seemed pleased with what we'd accomplished, which resulted in a fairly good bonus.

'Dog-Alley' – HOYLAKE Promenade (MEOLS Parade).

The day after finishing the sand, I walked into the messroom wondering what I'd be on.

Taffy managed to drag his eyes away from page three. When he saw me he bellowed "Why, if it isn't the Scottish Arab! Had a good sand dance, Haggis?"

"Get back to the bristlers on page three, Taffy." I advised him "Anyway if I'd the money that most of these Arabs have, I wouldn't need to come here and listen to your inane chatter!"

"What's inane, Haggis?" Cowboy quizzed.

I laughed "Ask Tom," I said, nodding to the cloud of smoke in the corner "he'll tell you."

Taking the pipe out of his mouth, Tom turned to the Cowboy "It just means devoid of any rational comprehension."

"Gerraway!" Cowboy murmured, while Taffy just sat behind his paper and glowered.

The messroom gradually filled and the bin wagons went out as they were crewed up. When all the binnies had gone, I looked round to see who were left. The Beak hadn't turned in, so there were only the Bear, Tom, Skinny and myself.

The Bear handed me a card "On your way, Jock." he barked in his sergeant major's voice.

I took the card, saluted and said "Yes sir."

He gave me such a glare, I scarpered fast!

Picking up my gear from the shed, I set off through the streets with my little green cart.

The card was round five, day five, so it took some time before I arrived at the territory. I almost managed to sweep one complete street before it was time to go to the bowling green hut for tea-break. I was just finishing my second cup when Frank, the green keeper came in.

"Hello Haggis, on this end today?" he asked as he brewed up from his constantly boiling kettle on the gas ring.

"Yeah, and it's harder work pushing that silly cart from the yard to here than it is sweeping the streets!"

He sat down at the table "Have another cuppa, I've got a full pot here."

Patting my belly, I said "I've downed two mugs already, I'm likely to burst!"

He held up a tin "I've got some conny-onny."

I laughed "Alright, you win. I can't resist that, fill us up."

I had another two cups with Frank and began to feel a bit bloated.

"What, with the heat and all this tea, I'm going to sweat cobs today." I grunted.

Getting myself pulled together, I got started again and managed to clean up half the streets on the card then made my way back to the yard, picking up flotsam and jetsam on the way.

Most of us probably don't completely understand how the urinary system works, but we all feel it's pressing needs at one time or another. That was how I felt now — in other words, I needed a piss badly!

As there were no public toilets on my route back to the yard, I had three choices; do it in the street, up a jigger, or go into a pub and use the toilet there.

Not liking the idea of being seen and being reported for indecent exposure, I chose the pub. The nearest one was the Railway Inn, so I headed there at a jog-trot.

It was a great relief to get rid of four cups of tea, and I was feeling much better as I walked out the door, but the feeling didn't last long. The Bear was slowly cruising past in his van and he was looking straight at me. I had just time to see his eyebrows. They were doing a tribal dance, and that was bad!

'Nothing to worry about, I've done nothing wrong.' I said to myself as I trundled back to the yard.

As I sauntered past the Bear's window, the tune that I was whistling froze on my lips . . . "Jock! Office!" he roared at me before I'd time to park the cart.

Again I found myself on the carpet facing the manager and the Bear. The manager put on his stern look, pursed his lips and said "Mister Carson says that he actually saw you coming out of a public house in working hours!"

I put on my disdainful look, held my head up and replied "Yes sir, that's perfectly correct."

Mister Howard must've been taking lessons from the Bear,

because his eyebrows shot up. "You can be sacked for drinking on duty!" he exclaimed.

"That might be true," I retorted "but I wasn't drinking on duty, in fact I wasn't drinking at all!"

His eyes narrowed "Well then, did you just go in for a look around?"

"Not exactly," I replied "I went in to satisfy the functions of nature!"

He leaned forward and with a supercilious look, said "You mean you were thirsty and needed a pint?"

I sighed "No, I only went into the pub to use the toilet, I had a lot of tea."

"That figures." muttered the Bear.

The manager was now looking perplexed. He scratched his head "Well," he said "you obviously don't smell of drink, but the fact remains that being in a public house during working hours is an offence. We'll give you another warning. Don't do it again!"

"That's fine," I said sarcastically "but when I started here, Mister Carson said that he, and I suppose he meant as representative of management, would do the thinking for me. So I humbly ask what I should do if I'm caught short on that two and a half mile stretch again?"

Once more Mister Howard scratched his head and dandruff began falling on the desk like snow. I watched fascinated, then when he saw me looking, he stopped scratching and turned in his seat and addressed the Bear imploringly "What do you think?"

The inspector's eyebrows were doing a jig. "On occasions like that you should use your own initiative!" he growled at me.

I played the game with gusto and raised my eyebrows "I did! That's why I'm here now!"

The Bear was getting decidedly agitated "Are you trying to put us on the spot, Mister Mackenzie?" he asked, hissing the words through clenched teeth.

Trying on my most innocent expression, I replied "No sir, you've put me on the carpet!"

He glared as if he would like to hit me "Drink less tea, is my suggestion!"

With mock astonishment I said "Are you denying me my tea-break, Mister Carson?"

He stabbed a finger at me and roared "I didn't say that!"

The manager was now getting really confused "Gentlemen, calm down! There must be a solution."

"Well," I said "there are two pubs on the . . . "

"You can't go into a public house during working hours!" the Bear said emphatically.

The manager, still perplexed, caused another little shower of dandruff as he searched for an answer "Leave it with us, Mister Mackenzie and we'll try to resolve this problem to everyone's satisfaction." he said with a tremendous sigh.

Feeling that I was in a better position now, I demanded "What about that warning?"

"A-a-ah," he stammered "we'll withdraw that. Thank you very much Mister Mackenzie, you can go now."

I turned and left the office, the manager still scattering dandruff on his desk. I laughed as I imagined the blizzard if the Bear's moustache and eyebrows caught the dandruff from Mister Howard!

As I walked into the messroom, Taffy put his paper down. He looked around to see if he had a good listening audience, then turned to me with a smirk "Trying to get the manager's job, boyo? You're in there often enough ! Won't do you any good though, that job'll go too!"

"Taffy," I said "did you hear about the little short-sighted Welsh girl who became a harpoonist on a whaler?"

"No-o-o" he said, eyeing me quizzically "let's have it."

"Oh it's not much," I murmured "it's just that she won the Miss Whales competition!"

"Ha-ha-ha." came the mock laugh "I bet they don't miss you in Scotland!"

After dinner break I emptied the muck out of the cart and again headed for the round. The streets were fairly clean, so it was an easy afternoon. For once I managed all the streets on the card, so I went back to the yard quite satisfied that the work had been completed.

The Bear was standing by the stores as I came in the gate. He stopped me, lifted the lid and looked in the cart. He put the lid back down and growled "Not much in there, have you just been strolling around, thisavvy?"

I sighed at the injustice of it "No, I haven't, If there's muck out there, I'll get it. If there's none, I can't bring it in. It's logical, as Spock would say!"

He squinted at me and barked "On your way, Captain Kirk!"

I docked the cart and made the trek home to the star of my life — the wife!

The Binmen are Coming

Chapter 6

ON THE BINS

On the third Monday in July it looked like it was going to be a scorcher. Walking into the messroom, I saw that most of the men were engrossed in the morning papers.

Looking around I proclaimed to all and sundry "Good morning everyone — and Taffy."

Cowboy muttered "'morning" into his paper without lifting his eyes from page three.

Andy Cap gave me a quizzical look "Why does Taffy get a special mention?" he asked.

Laughing, I replied "He's a good friend of mine, life for me wouldn't be the same without Taffy!"

Taffy managed to drag his eyes away from the buxom bosom in his paper "With a friend like you, who needs enemies!" he retorted.

"Come off it Taffy!" I exclaimed "I'm a butt for your banter. You enjoy the repartee!"

With a bemused expression the little Welshman turned to the Cowboy "What's this Scottish twit talking about?" he asked irritably.

His mentor looked pensive "Something about enjoying butties at a party, I think!" he drawled, tilting his chair back and pushing his hat away from his forehead.

"Greedy pig, he's always thinking about his belly!" Taffy muttered, returning his eyes and thoughts to the bristlers on page three.

Old Tom was sitting in the corner chortling "Sit yourself down Haggis, your erudition is wasted in here. I told you before, if they cut out swear words they'd be dumb!"

I gave him the thumbs up "Thanks Tom."

The Bear was surveying the scene "You sound as if you're fit today, Jock." he said, matter-of-factly.

"Fit as a fiddle" I replied "but I'm glad I'm not on the bins, it'll be murder with this heat!"

A supercilious smile came on his face, perfected by plenty of practice "Wrong again Jock, Rooster's on holiday and you're taking his place."

"Not round three!" I moaned.

"Right first time!" he affirmed, savouring my consternation with glee.

I uttered my strongest expletive "Good Gordon Highlanders!"

Cowboy looked up with a grin "I love these cuss-words you use, Haggis." he said, repeating the words and rolling them round his tongue.

"They're not swear words, they're substitutes!" I countered.

"Bloody hell Haggis, you could've fooled me. They sound great, I've heard you use 'em before."

The Bear broke in "You're crewed up Cowboy, on your way."

"Wagons roll boys," Cowboy drawled, then turning towards me, added "and bring your Gordon Highlanders, Haggis, you'll need 'em today!"

The crew trooped out to the wagon, Cowboy leading the way. I climbed into the back seat over an old battery, a wall clock, and stubbed my toe on an old rusty lawnmower before I could sit down.

When we got to Greasby the wagon stopped to let the truckers out. Billy opened the door and jumped out. Taffy sat still, thoroughly engrossed in his paper.

Cowboy glared at him and barked "C'mon short-arse, move yer body, you're trucking this week!"

Taffy jumped, rolled up the paper, shoved it into his pocket and stumbled over the junk in the cab.

Cowboy rolled his eyes "You been on the bubbly last night?" he growled at him.

Taffy glared back at the Cowboy "No boyo, just practicing a dance step!"

"Thought the Welsh were singers, not dancers!" I said.

He paused at the door "We're the greatest singers and the best dancers in the world. The Welsh can do anything!"

"Bum!" Cowboy spat out, putting his foot on Taffy's bottom and giving him a push out of the door.

As the wagon lurched forward he turned to me "Little twat gets up yer nose sometimes but he's a great worker."

A few streets on, the wagon stopped and the rest of us got out. For the first couple of streets we had to pull out the full bins and tip them till we caught up with the truckers.

Going up one path, I tried to lift the bin. It was heavy as lead so I dragged it out. It made a loud screech as I sledged it along the path. A window opened and a plumpish woman hung out and roared "Don't do that, you'll scrape t'bottom!"

I looked up at her filling the window frame and shouted back "It'll get rid of some of your barnacles!"

"Cheek," she squealed "we'll get better service when the private firm takes over!"

Tapping my chest, I declared "I am a private citizen."

"Oh no you're not," she roared back "you're council, and rubbish at that!"

"At least I haven't got barnacles!" I retorted.

She let out a howl like a jigger-rabbit on the tiles and banged the window down so hard that a neighbour rushed out thinking that our wagon had crashed.

Cowboy and I had to double up to tip the bin into the wagon, it was so heavy.

"Haggis," Cowboy said "when they're as heavy as this, just leave 'em. If you keep lifting bins like this, you'll get ruptures not barnacles!"

"O.K., will do." I said.

"Another thing," he declared "don't spit in this area!"

"Why?" I asked "It seems like the right place to spit. It looks a broken down district."

"So are some of the people."

"Why shouldn't I spit, then?" I demanded to know.

"Haggis, they'll steal your spit before it ever reaches the ground!"

"That bad, eh?" I said with a laugh, wondering how much he was exaggerating.

Just then a police car roared past, siren wailing.

Cowboy was about to comment when I held up my hand "Say no more," I said "I see what you mean!"

A couple of hours later the temperature had risen into the seventies. I started to sweat like a pig.

After a while Cowboy remarked "It's early finish today, Haggis, what'll you do with yourself?"

"Well," I replied, smacking my lips "I'll get a pint of my home brew and laze in the Irish garden!"

Silence — the Cowboy was thinking.

"You got an Irish garden?" he quizzed.

"Yup."

Another silence . . .

He tipped another two bins, then as he put them down, said "Never heard of that. What's an Irish garden?"

"A padio!" I replied, trying to keep a straight face.

His laughter was loud and rich "Bloody hell Haggis, you mean a patio!"

"That's what I said."

"I must tell that to the wife tonight. Where d'you get 'em Haggis?"

Tipping another heavy bin, I grunted "I read comic-cuts."

Again he laughed heartily "You got good taste in reading, then."

It had been a hard day. With the heat and the heavy bins, I must've lost a few pints of sweat. All was going well though until about half an hour before we finished. Billy and Taffy had finished trucking and had come back to join us. Jim Lad and Andy Cap had also appeared on the scene. My next bin was another heavy one.

"Taffy," I shouted over "can you give me a punt with this swine?"

He hoisted it onto my shoulder. It was full of wet stuff and the side of the bin was split. Before I could tip it into the wagon, a slurry of foul smelling gunge cascaded down my neck.

"Hell's bells!" I shrieked, tipping the muck into the wagon and throwing the empty back at the gate.

"Temper, temper." Taffy said mockingly "D'ye want me to pick the maggots off your collar, boyo?"

"Get 'em off!" I shouted "I'm liable to get beri-beri or yurs or something!"

"I'll buy you a pint when we finish, Haggis." Taffy said consolingly.

"A pint!" I screamed "It's penicillin I need!"

"I think you've just got some down the back of your neck!" Cowboy said, shaking with laughter.

Livid with rage I was dancing around, dabbing at my collar "I'm going to sue somebody!" I lamented.

"You've dented her bin Haggis." Billy exclaimed "She might sue you."

"To pot with her," I said in exasperation "I stink!"

Taffy grinned "Don't worry, Haggis. You're not that bad, we're still your friends."

When the last bin went back, we all climbed into the wagon. I was the last one in, me and about twenty thousand flies buzzing round my head.

It had really made Taffy's day. I'd never seen him so happy. He was sitting grinning from ear to ear "Looks like you've been baptised Haggis, you're a real binman now!"

"Do you like me now that I smell, Taffy?"

He pinched his nose between his fingers "Boyo, you smell the same as you always did!"

"Don't think so Taffy," I said, sniffing my shirt "it smells like Chili Con Carne."

The wagon rocked with the laughter.

When we were almost home, Cowboy said to Jack, the driver "Drop me and Haggis off at the Ship."

"O.K.," Jack replied as he knocked a few more chips off the gears.

Alighting at the Ship Inn, we went in and marched up to the bar. The barman was eyeing us strangely as he sniffed the air. "I'm going to lose customers with you lot coming in here!" he lamented.

Cowboy was most indignant "What d'you mean? We're nice people!" he asserted, looking very hurt.

The barman spread his hands "I don't doubt that" he said "but you don't smell nice. Why don't you go home and wash and change first?"

Cowboy looked grieved "It's now we need a pint! Anyway, it's just that Haggis had a slight accident."

Screwing up his nose, the barman growled "There's nobody in the snug, go in there and I'll bring your pints through."

"O.K., let's do that then Cowboy," I said "anything for a quiet life."

Once we'd downed a couple of pints each, I said "I'm off now Cowboy."

He laughed "You can say that again. You smell rich."

I groaned "Ha ha, I'm going home for a bath. I'll see you in the morning."

"O.K., See you, Haggis."

As I walked home I got a few stares and funny looks from passers by. The best reaction though, was yet to come.

When I walked in the back door, Blodwyn and Moira, our two boxer bitches nearly bowled me over. They jumped all over me, sniffing and smelling, wagging their tails like mad.

"Well, at least all this gunge is appreciated by you two." I said as I tried to keep them from knocking me down.

Stripping off all my clothes, I stood in the nuddie and watched the two dogs rolling about and having a good time on my reeking duds on the floor.

I was enjoying the show when Jane walked in. She took one look at me standing there with nothing on "Good grief," she spluttered "you'd better get out of the way or the dogs'll think I've brought them a bone from the butchers!"

Blowing her a raspberry, I said "Very funny, I'm just going to pop into the bath before you think about making soup!"

She came over and started stroking my flesh "Your manly body odour's turning me on," she said with a grin "can I come in and sponge you down?"

"Gerroff! You're sex mad woman!" I squawked, making a dash for the safety of the bathroom.

"Spoil-sport!" she shouted after me "A woman could get a divorce for less!"

"Quiet, woman. I've got a headache." I said, and just had time to close the bathroom door before one of my boots hit it with a bang.

I really enjoyed the bath. It was lovely to be clean again. After a brisk rub down with a towel, I glowed all over. When I walked into the bedroom, I found Jane sitting waiting for me with a large glass of whisky in her hand. She held it out to me with a smile "Here Steve, have a reviver, you've had a hard day."

Taking the glass, I had a sip "What's on your little mind?" I asked her with suspicion.

"Nothing like that!" she purred "It's just that I've invited Jeff and Gloria over for a game of Trivial Pursuit."

" Hell's bells," I yelled "no wonder you plied me with drink. Why them? They always win, can't you invite somebody we can beat?"

She laughed "It makes them feel good, and they always bring a bottle of wine."

"Yeah," I said, taking another sip of the whisky "but they always drink most of it themselves."

Jane stood up "Be sociable Steve — but not TOO much! Put some clothes on before they arrive!"

We had a good game, in fact it went better than I thought it would. We played pairs, Jane and me against Gloria and Jeff. After an hour it was pretty even. We had five wedges and so had they. Then came a winning streak for us. I threw the dice and our token landed in blue.

Jeff asked the question "What Indian City is served by Dum Dum Airport?" he read with a smirk.

"Calcutta." I replied quickly.

He scowled "How d'you know that?"

"We've been around." I replied while Jane tittered.

Our next throw landed us in the green category headquarters. It was the last wedge we needed.

Again Jeff read the question "What tusked creature helped embellish sailors' tales of unicorns?"

Confidently I stated "The narwhal."

Jeff glared at me "I don't believe this!" he snarled.

Gloria was livid, she squealed "They've memorised all the answers!"

We ignored them and carried on the game, reaching the hub in no time at all, thus winning the game.

Gloria's face was grim. Pointing her thumb at her husband, she exclaimed "He won't live this down you know, being beaten at Trivial Pursuit by a binman and his wife!"

Jeff gulped down the last dregs of the cheap red wine they had brought with them. The sound was magnified by the heavy silence that had ensued after Gloria's remark.

Her eyes were bleak, but Jane's were sparking. Glaring at Gloria, she demanded "What's wrong with binmen? And their wives for that matter?"

Gloria cocked her snoot in the air and retorted acidly "You must admit that binmen aren't very far up the social ladder, if in fact they're on it at all!"

Jane retaliated "My Steve works beside a teacher at the depot, and anyway your Jeff isn't even working!"

Gloria was furious "Jeff's not working because he refuses these common jobs that are offered to him!"

Jeff hiccuped and muttered "We'd better go, Gloria."

As they left, Gloria was still chunnering going out the door.

"That's the last time they'll be here!" Jane announced as she slammed the door behind them.

"Thank goodness for that." I said, heading for the bedroom.

I slept soundly that night.

Chapter 7

ON THE CARPET AGAIN

In the morning I got up and made myself a big plate of lumpy porridge. Washing that down with a mug of strong char, I got ready for work. As I was going out the door, I could hear the dawn chorus — No, it wasn't the birds! It was Jane, Blodwyn and Moira snoring their heads off.

"Longer they sleep the less they'll eat." I muttered as I headed for the yard.

Walking into the messroom I was greeted by Taffy's dulcet tones "You smell sweet this morning Haggis. Had your yearly bath, have you?"

I smiled demurely at him "My nature's sweet too, Taffy. I don't provoke."

He looked at me in disbelief "Bloody hell boyo, you seen the light or something?"

I ignored that and had a look round to see what crews were in. Round three was the first gang to be complete this morning for a change, so Cowboy spoke up "Our lot's all here, Jim."

"O.K., on your way then." barked the Bear.

Billy stood up, stuck his thumbs in his belt and chanted "Wagons roll, boys."

Cowboy caught him by the scruff and shook him till his teeth rattled "Listen you," he bawled in poor Billy's ear "when you're charge-hand you can say that. Not before!"

"Sorry." Billy said, squirming free and rubbing the back of his neck.

We clattered out to the wagon and with a lot of shouting and doors banging we were off. Round three might be the best gang work-wise, but it certainly wasn't the quietest!

There was a three mile stretch of country road to travel before we reached Greasby. Just as we entered the first long straight, we spied a young girl on her own, walking in the same direction, going towards Greasby. She wore a mini-skirt which gave everyone a good view of strong fleshy thighs. There was plenty of pink flesh bulging out of other places as well.

Young Jim Lad's face was glued to the window, his eyes protruding like organ stops. "I'd have that!" he growled as he drooled at the thought.

"You wouldn't know what to do with it if you had it!" Billy said, laughing.

"Bloody don't you believe it, just give me half a chance!" Jim Lad asserted, his eyeballs nearly touching the glass.

Before you could say 'Jack Robinson', Billy, Taffy and Andy Cap had grabbed Jim Lad and dragged his trousers off, while trying to avoid his flailing arms and legs.

Taffy rolled down the window fully on the near side and Billy threw the trousers out.

"Bloody pigs!" roared Jim Lad as he lunged at the door and tried to jump out while the wagon was thundering along.

"Hell's bells," Cowboy shouted at the top of his voice "stop the bloody wagon, Jack."

The wagon shuddered to a halt as Jack stood on the brakes, but it must've been about a hundred yards from where Jim's trousers had gone out the window. Jim Lad jumped out and ran back to retrieve his good working kecks. I jumped down as well to see what was happening. The Cowboy, Billy, Andy Cap and Taffy all hung out the window. Taffy was shouting at the top of his lungs "Go get 'er, boyo!"

Imagine what the girl saw — a wild young man with tousled hair and no trousers on, running towards her with a gleam in his eye.

Her eyes went wide, her mouth dropped open, then she did a pirouette that would've pleased a top ballerina. Without even a glance round she took to her heels and started running hell for leather back the way she'd come, screaming at the top of her voice.

Jim Lad grabbed his trousers, scrambled into them and ran back to the wagon.

We hauled him in panting, as Taffy said "Didn't make it then boyo, did you?"

Jim Lad gasped out "Pigs!" and collapsed into a seat.

"Bloody hell lads," Cowboy groaned "I smell trouble!"

GREASBY stretch (between NEWTON and FRANKBY).

Billy turned to face him with a puzzled expression "What trouble? He didn't touch her!"

Cowboy was adamant "He'd no trousers on, he could be charged with indecent exposure!"

Billy frowned "She probably didn't see anything she hasn't seen before!" he argued.

It didn't convince the Cowboy. "That's not the point!" he bawled at Billy "You wait, the Bear'll be out later." then to the driver he said "Carry on Jack."

The usual crashing of gears and we were off again with the wagon lurching forward in leaps and bounds.

Cowboy tapped the driver on the back "Fill up with Aussie petrol this morning did you, Jack?" he asked as we swayed back and forth.

Jack retorted "It's diesel!"

"It still feels like kangaroo stuff." Cowboy muttered.

Jack's feelings were hurt "It's the mechanics," he lamented "they haven't repaired the clutch properly, it's sticking a bit."

We trundled on and eventually reached Greasby and started our round. When we'd worked for about an hour, Jim Lad came back and fished out the black tea-pot and walked off.

"Where does he make the tea today?" I asked the Cowboy as I tipped a heavy bin full of glass bottles.

"Lady in the next street makes it every Tuesday." he roared, vying with the crashing glass to make himself heard.

"That's good of her." I said.

"Yeah, it's handy. We give all five ladies who make the tea, a box of chocolates every Christmas."

I laughed "That's a new one, binmen giving the householders a tip!"

"It's worth it Haggis, to get boiling water for our tea every morning."

We'd worked for about half an hour after tea-break when the Bear drove up in his van.

Cowboy stopped tipping when he walked up. "Everything O.K., Jim?" he asked in greeting.

78

"No it bloody isn't" the Bear replied vehemently "It's a flaming mad gang you have, Cowboy. What have you done now?"

"He didn't touch her!" Cowboy protested.

"Only attempted rape then, is it?" the Bear rasped, his eyebrows starting to tango.

Cowboy kept up the defence of his men "It was only high spirits, you know what this lot are like."

"Don't I just!" the Bear said with a sigh "Anyway Mister Howard wants all the gang and the driver in the office when you come in at mid-day."

The charge-hand's brow was furrowed "Did she report it to the police?" he queried.

"I don't know," came the reply "but her father rang the manager, and he's not pleased."

The furrows on Cowboy's brow got deeper "Who's not pleased, her father?"

The Bear was snarling now "Don't try to be smart, Cowboy. All seven of you — in the office at the double when you get back to the yard!"

With that he stormed off, jumped into his van and drove away, tyres screeching. He seemed angry, because the last glimpse I got of him, it looked as though his eyebrows were starting a highland fling, and that was bad.

"That's all Taffy's fault." I said to Cowboy.

"Andy Cap and Billy helped it on a bit as well," he sighed "but we'll have to take whatever comes."

When we finished our mornings work we all got in the wagon and headed for the yard and our confrontation with the depot manager.

At the yard we congregated at the office door but nobody seemed anxious to go any further. Cowboy was pushed to the front. He knocked on the manager's door.

"Come in." roared the Bear from within.

Cowboy opened the door and we all filed in behind him and stood in front of the desk. Mister Howard sat behind the desk with the inspector in his usual position, standing at his left.

Mister Howard ran his eyes along the row of dirty scraggy binmen.

"I'm sorry there aren't enough chairs in here," he said "you'll all have to stand."

"That's alright." Cowboy replied, shifting from one foot to the other.

The manager's eyes came to rest on Jim Lad "Are you the one who had his trousers off?" he queried.

Jim Lad's eyes never left the floor "Yes sir." he said in a quiet voice.

The interrogator continued "Did you take them off yourself?"

"Yes sir." Jim said again, lying his head off, trying to be loyal to the gang.

Cowboy butted in "That's not true sir, the men took them off!"

The manager turned to face the speaker "Which men? Exactly who was responsible?"

Nobody spoke.

Finally the manager broke the silence "Well, if that's the way you want it," he said grimly "then all seven must bear the responsibility. If the punishment is to be sacking, then all seven of you will be sacked!"

I could see that Billy was getting worried. "It was only a bit of a lark, sir." he protested.

"A lark!" the manager retorted "It's very serious, if the girl informs the police, Jim could be charged with indecent exposure and attempted rape. You other six would be charged with aiding and abetting!"

Andy Cap's face was a picture of anxiety "Can we say that we're sorry?" he cajoled.

"I'm afraid it's too late for apologies," came the grim reply "at the moment I'll do three things. Firstly, all seven will lose one day's bonus. Secondly, all of you are severely reprimanded. Thirdly, take a severe warning that if anything like it ever happens again, the culprit will be sacked. If the culprit doesn't own up, then the whole crew, including the driver will be sacked!"

There was silence while everybody digested that.

Cowboy spoke up "Thank you sir, is that all?"

The reply was emphatic "No it isn't! There is one proviso!"

"What's that sir?" asked the Cowboy.

Mister Howard looked along the row at each of us and said "If the girl changes her mind and goes to the police, you could all be charged. If and when that happens, you will all be sacked. So your jobs depend on what the girl does!"

The Bear had stood through the whole proceedings and hadn't said a word. Mister Howard turned to him now and said "Have you anything to add, Mister Carson?"

"No sir, you dealt with it very well." replied the Bear, pursing his lips and looking disdainfully at the motley crew standing in front of the desk.

The manager seemed pleased with that. Turning back to us, he said "You can go now gentlemen."

We all trooped out sadder but wiser men, at least I was.

Dinner break over, we headed back to Greasby. On the same stretch we saw another young girl walking towards the village.

I could hardly believe my ears, for Jim Lad was beginning to growl again. Immediately Cowboy grabbed him, shook him like a rat and roared in his ear "Listen twat, any more of that and I'll personally throw you out and leave you there!"

Jim Lad squirmed loose "Haven't you any love in your body?" he lamented.

Cowboy retorted "That's not love with you, it's pure lust!"

The lad was sitting there so dejected, I began to feel a bit sorry for him "Jim" I said "why don't you get a nice young girl and marry her?"

He pouted and exclaimed "I am trying!"

"That's not the way to go about it, growling and ogling the girls." I said with a grin.

Turning to face me, he raised his voice to be heard above the roar of the engine "What's the right way, then?"

"Well," I replied "make a date with a young lady, get a romance going. Take her to the pictures. Read her some poetry in the park, that still turns them on you know!"

He replied with a frown "Don't know any poems Haggis, do you?"

Taffy stuck his oar in "Don't use any of Haggis' poems, the birds wouldn't understand Rabbie Burns!"

I laughed "You're wrong Taffy. Burns is known all over the world.

Even the Russians read his poems. Didn't you know that?"

"Bloody hell boyo," the Welshman replied "can you imagine a big Russian reciting a poem in a Scottish accent. It could start world war three!"

"Taffy," I replied "It's more likely to start in the hills and valleys of Wales if they're all like you down there!"

"You must be joking, Haggis!" he exclaimed "Look at your own history, the clans up there used to slaughter one another if they didn't like the colour of one another's tartan kilt!"

"Taffy, never mind arguing about past history, wars and the land of your mothers . . ."

"Fathers!" he interjected.

"Well, whatever it is. We want something happy and loving for Jim Lad."

"How about a nice Welsh song?" Taffy suggested.

"Don't think so." I replied "Some of Burns' poems though, would be very good for wooing. There's one about a red rose, it's a lovely one. I'll write it out for you tonight Jim and bring it in tomorrow."

"Thanks Haggis, I'll learn it by heart." he replied with a grin.

"Watch it though, Jim," I said "once the girls hear your recitation, they'll all be after you!"

"That'll suit me fine." he said, eyes twinkling.

The wagon shuddered to a halt bringing us back to reality. We had arrived at our starting point. Everyone separated to their various tasks and I was left to tip with Cowboy.

Once they'd gone, he said "It's a flaming mad gang this one, Haggis, but they're all good workers. This round's got the best bonus of the three, so that makes up for quite a lot, don't ye think?"

Lifting a bin and tipping it, I replied above the din of the crusher "Yeah, I don't mind working hard and I like the bonus, but they seem to attract trouble!"

Cowboy grunted as he got a heavy one this time. He tipped the rubbish and dropped the empty bin with a clatter. "That's true," he replied "they work hard and play hard, but the play does get a bit rough at times, I must admit."

Just then the wagon from round one thundered past. The driver gave us the thumbs down.

"What's wrong with him?" I asked "and where's he been?"

Cowboy laughed "He's on his way back from the tip. Thumbs down means that the Bear's on the prowl, so you'd better look busy, Haggis."

I could hardly believe my ears "Look busy!" I bellowed "Good grief, my back's broken with work and you say 'look busy'!"

"You'll get used to it." he said "By the end of September it'll be a doddle."

"You're joking, I'll be off this and back on the brush when Rooster comes back."

Cowboy laughed again "That's what you think. Three of the gang have got to get their two weeks holiday yet and some might take their other week in the summer as well. So I guess you'll be with us for some time."

"Good Gordon Highlanders!"

"What's the matter, Haggis? Don't you like us?"

"No it's not that, I just didn't expect it so soon, to be on the bins for that long, I mean."

"Never mind, think of the ackers you'll be coining in!"

"Yeah that's true, I think I'll buy a car. You got one, Cowboy?"

"Yeah, but it's three years old now, I'm thinking of trading it in for a new one."

I said, half to myself and half to Cowboy "I think Jane and I could go on holiday abroad. Maybe put a mortgage on a house and get out of the council house we're in."

Cowboy was serious now "Don't do anything silly, Haggis! Remember you could be made redundant any day!"

"Yeah, I'd forgotton about that, but it seems never . . ."

The crash woke me from my daydreaming. One of the teeth of the crusher had caught the bin I'd been tipping.

"Yipes. . ." I yelled, kicking the stop-bar. "the bin's got jammed!"

"Don't worry, Haggis." Cowboy said as he thumped the reverse lever and the teeth rolled upwards and released the bin. He pulled it out and dropped it on the ground. The nice round bin had now been squashed into an oval shape!

I looked at it in dismay "Good grief, will they dock my wages for the price of a new bin?"

He laughed heartily "Look Haggis." he said and took the bin and turned it on it's side with the oval pointing upwards.

"Hold it there." he said to me and then stood on it, pushing it back into an almost round shape.

"There's still a dent in it!" I lamented as I examined the bin.

Putting his foot inside it, he said "You worry too much, Haggis." and kicked the dent out!

He threw the bin to me "There y'are, charge her for a new bin." then roared "Hi-e-up" to the driver.

The wagon lurched to the next set of bins. A lady wearing gardening gloves was waiting by the gate. She shouted over "Could you take a few bags of garden rubbish."

Cowboy went over and I heard him say "I'm very sorry, it's against the rules to take garden rubbish."

She looked peeved "Oh I see," she said "couldn't you bend the rules a little? Would a couple of quid help?"

Cowboy's face took on a benign expression, and without any hesitation replied "Yes of course, we'll take them this time. We're always willing to help a lady in distress."

We threw in her bags of garden rubbish and then two pounds changed hands. Cowboy put one in his pocket and gave me the other.

"Don't you share the tips with the gang?" I asked him.

"Yes, at Christmas time we do. All tips go into the kitty then, but any small ones through the year we just put in our skyrocket."

When we were almost finished, the same thing happened. This time it was a man who was waiting for us.

"Can you take some garden rubbish?" he asked, indicating a few plastic bags by the gate.

Again Cowboy's reply came "Sorry, against the rules!"

"It could be worth it." he said as he jingled money in his pocket.

"Sorry!" Cowboy said emphatically, then shouted "Hi-e-up." and the wagon lumbered forward to the next set of bins.

Further along the road I said to Cowboy "Good grief, why didn't you take that man's garden rubbish? He was going to give us a tip!"

"Wrong Haggis, he wouldn't you know. Never ever be caught by a money jingler. Those coins will never leave his pocket, in tips anyway!"

"How do you know?" I quizzed.

Cowboy gave me a paternal look "I've been on this job about twenty years and I know all the tricks. I don't mind helping people, but watch out for his kind, they wouldn't give you last night's Echo!"

I laughed "I'm glad I took this job, it's giving me a good insight into human nature in the various echelons of society."

"Bloody hell Haggis," he said as he nearly hit my toe with a bin "what kind of society is that?"

"It just means the different strata."

"Do you mean the rich and the poor?" he asked.

"Thinking about it, I suppose it boils down in the long run to how much money you have or haven't got."

"Why didn't you say that, Haggis? You're as bad as old Tom!"

"Yeah," I said "he's a character. I like Tom, it's a real education working with him."

"He's the last of his kind, I reckon." Cowboy mused.

"Not with you around!" I retorted, and had to duck the bin he threw at me.

At last the truckers came back as we had reached the end of the day's work. When the last bin was tipped we all went back to help put the empties away.

As we were getting into the wagon Taffy said "Another day, another dollar, Haggis."

"Hope I get more than a dollar for today's work!" I said wearily.

"You must be worth a mint!" he replied.

"I'm not even worth the hole in the middle." I said.

When we got back to the yard, Cowboy said "Going for a bevvy, Haggis?"

"You buying?"

"Yeah sure," he replied with a laugh "I'll buy the first one and you buy the rest."

"Not a good deal," I said "but I'll come anyway."

When we walked into the Ship Inn, the barman said in a loud voice "Here come the smellies in their wellies!"

"Our money's welcome, isn't it?" I retorted "Even though we're not. Anyway we're not wearing wellies!"

"What'll you have?" the barman asked with a scowl.

The Cowboy ordered "Two pints of best bitter."

He drew the beer, gave Cowboy his change and said "There y'are lads, I'll just turn on the extractor fan, it'll give us a change of air at least."

Glaring at him, I said "You insinuating something?"

"No — no," he replied "but people might think that the beer's gone off."

"They might be right!" Cowboy remarked, sipping his pint.

The barman gave him his best scowl "If you don't like it," he growled "I can recommend another pub you could go to!"

"No, we'll stay. We like the smell in here." Cowboy said, sniffing the air.

"You're the only ones!" the barman muttered, stalking off to serve someone who'd just come in.

We sank a couple of pints after that, then I made my way home. Jane met me at the door. "You're coming home earlier every day!! Are you sure you're going to work?"

"That's a fine welcome," I said "give us a kiss."

She kissed me then pushed me back "You've been drinking!" she squealed.

"Two pints isn't drinking." I argued.

"It's drinking alright. You're taking me out tonight for a drink or else no go . . . ."

"You can't do that, you know it's the law that a man's got his rights!"

"Male chauvinist pig!" she cried and kicked my ankle.

"Alright," I said, rubbing my ankle "we'll go to a pub . . ."

"No!" she said "I want to go to a club, what about the Country Club?"

"Good grief, have you seen the prices there?"

"Yes," she replied "but it's more romantic and we can have a dance and a smooch."

"I don't like smooching in public!"

"That's what I get for marrying a binman." she said with a sigh.

"I wasn't a binman when we got married. Anyway, get your glad-rags on, it's the Country Club tonight!"

She gave me a hug and a kiss . . .

Chapter 8

COW AND GATE

...In the morning I was tired. Dragging myself out of bed, I had a quick breakfast and headed for the yard.

When I walked into the messroom it was already crowded and the hubbub was louder than usual. Nobody was looking at their paper, everyone seemed to be talking at once.

It wasn't long before I knew what all the talk was about. Frank, the chargehand from round one, who was also our shop-steward looked up "Half four tonight, Haggis!" he said like he was giving an order.

"Yeah, I'll be sitting with my feet up by that time!" I replied just as cockily.

"No you won't." he retorted sharply, sounding just like the Bear "you'll be here in the messroom for a union meeting!"

My heart sank "Oh no, you're not calling a strike, are you?"

He replied with great officiousness "We're protecting your job! We're trying to block this move towards privatization."

"Alright, I may deign to be present!" I said haughtily, just to show that I didn't like his overbearing attitude.

Getting the final word in, Frank said grimly "You'd better be here!"

The Bear broke in "You're crewed up, Frank. On your way."

Round one went out, quickly followed by round two.

"You're still short of one." the inspector said to Cowboy.

"Yeah, Andy Cap's not usually late, so it looks as if he's off for the day."

The Bear's eyebrows were waltzing "You'd better pick up the yob from West Kirby."

The Cowboy looked worried "Bloody hell, Jim, can't we have a sweeper from here?"

"No you can't, I'm short of men today. It's either the yob or you work with five men. Take your choice!"

"O.K., we'll pick him up on our way." Cowboy said without any enthusiasm "Wagons roll, boys."

We all clattered out the messroom and climbed aboard the wagon. Turning to Billy, I asked "Why do they call him the yob?"

He laughed "I thought you would know that, Haggis. Yob is boy backwards, so he's a backward boy."

"Oh, I see," I said "will he be any use?"

Scratching his head, he replied "No, probably not, I think we would've been better with five men. The bonus would be bigger for one thing."

We picked up the sweeper at the bothy in West Kirby. His name was Sammy and nobody dared call him yob within hearing distance. He wasn't a bright lad, but he was big and strong. 'He'll be handy to lift heavy bins.' I thought.

When we reached Greasby we dropped off Taffy and Billy to start pulling the bins out. Driving on another two streets we got to our starting point. Cowboy, Jim Lad, Sammy and I all jumped out. Cowboy turned to Jim Lad "Jim, you and Sammy take back, but truck a few till we get a start."

"O.K." Jim said, and to Sammy "Pull out the full ones on that side with me."

Cowboy was tipping two at a time. As he turned from the wagon he saw Sammy walk past a gate without going in.

"Sammy! — You missed one!" Cowboy shouted.

"Yer wha?" enquired Sammy.

"Get that gate!" roared the Cowboy.

"Aw right."

Cowboy took his two empties back and as he turned, he was just in time to see that Sammy had gone to the one that he'd missed, lifted the small wrought-iron gate bodily off its hinges and had thrown it into the wagon!

Cowboy's face was a picture. His mouth dropped open and his eyes had come out further than Jim Lad's when he had seen the girl on the Frankby stretch.

From a standing start, I reckon he would've clocked about 0-60 m.p.h. in ten seconds flat. On his last step he kicked the stop-bar with a bang — and the teeth of the crusher just rested on the gate!

He thumped the reverse button and roared "What the bloody hell's fire d'yu think you're doing?"

Sammy scowled "You said 'get de gate!' "

"The bin! We're emptying bins! Not collecting scrap!" the Cowboy snarled, picking the gate out from among the refuse and carrying it back. He was having a little bit of trouble getting it back onto its hinges, so I went over to help.

We'd just got it into position when the householder came out. "What are you two doing?" she asked, with a quizzical expression on her face.

Cowboy looked a picture of innocence. Smiling at her, he said "We're into wrought-iron. We were only admiring your gate, it's a work of art!"

She gazed at us in complete bewilderment "Are you really serious?" she asked.

"Yes." Cowboy replied as we turned to go "It's a nice one, we"ll bring a camera next time and take a picture of it!"

When we went back to the wagon, everything had stopped. Jack, the driver had got out the cab to see what was going on. Cowboy had recovered quite a bit and to Sammy he asked quietly "What did you do that for?"

"I — I — tho — tho — the — ga — ga — te . . ." Sammy stuttered.

Cowboy was now back to normal. Looking at Sammy, he said "Spit it out on the footpath and I'll read it!"

Obediently, Sammy spat on the footpath!

Cowboy went over, leaned forward, looked at the spot where the boy had spat and said as if he were reading "I — thought — the — gate — was — to — go — on — the — wagon!"

Sammy looked at him in amazement.

We all roared with laughter. Even Sammy joined in. I was glad that the incident had ended on such a good note.

"I'll keep Sammy tipping here with me." Cowboy said "Haggis, you carry back with Jim Lad."

"That's fine with me." I said.

Jack went back to the cab and we started off again.

It was a doddle, taking back the empties. Much easier than tipping or trucking.

We'd worked for about an hour when Jim came over "Tea-time now Haggis." he said "Taffy makes the tea this morning, he'll have it ready by now."

"O.K." I said "I could go a cup. What d'yu think of the 'gate' lark this morning?"

"It could've been bad," he replied "but Cowboy has a way of making bad things funny in the end."

"Yeah, that was O.K., but he didn't manage it with your trouser episode, did he?"

"No, that's true, but I reckon it'll blow over. By the way, did you remember to write out my poem?"

"Yeah, it's in my jacket pocket in the wagon."

"Thanks Haggis." he said gleefully, as we trudged our way back to the wagon and tea-break. "Is it a long one?"

"No, it's only five verses, you should be able to memorise it quite easily."

We were the last two to arrive at the wagon. We climbed in the cab and I gave Jim Lad the poem. While he was reading it Taffy almost stuck his nose in my sarneys. "What's on yer butties today, Haggis, porridge?"

Dragging them away from under his drippy nose, I replied "No, it's chopped egg and chives."

"Gerraway! How d'yu make them?"

"S'easy, boil your egg for five minutes till it's hard, then take the shell off. Put the egg in a cup and chop it up with the chives. Put it on the bread and Bob's your uncle!" I said, taking a big bite at one and chewing like mad.

Taffy sniffed the air "Smell's good," he said "can I have one?"

"Can I try one as well?" Cowboy asked.

"I'd like one too!" Billy chimed in.

I looked at them all sitting gaping and drooling over my butties. "Good grief, if I give you all one, what am I going to eat?"

Cowboy laughed "Tit for tat, Haggis, we'll give you one each for one of yours!"

The exchanges took place. For my break, I had a red cheese butty, a jam butty and one with some sort of spread that looked like gunge from the back of the wagon!

Three of them were enjoying my nice chopped egg and chive butties while I was eating their rubbish!

Billy was chewing his with relish. He lifted the corner and peeked inside at the egg and chives. "Did your wife make these up?" he asked.

"Good Gordon Highlanders, you must be joking. Jane'll still be snoring." I replied.

Cowboy, through a mouthful of chopped egg said "Yu-um, it's great Haggis, you should be a chef."

"I wouldn't like that," I said, spitting out a piece of rind from the red cheese butty " the unsociable hours don't seem very good, I like an early finish. That's one of the attractions of the bins."

Taffy said "You mean you don't like work, Haggis! You stay at home and we'll bring your pay to the house. Would you like that?"

I laughed "No, I wouldn't like that either. A man should have a three way balance!"

Taffy was all ears "O.K., explain, Haggis." he said as the rest of them went quiet, waiting for some words of wisdom.

All that was heard now was the gentle chewing of brown bread butties and the faint aroma of chopped egg and chives.

I laughed "There's nothing mysterious about it. Firstly, a man needs work, but it musn't be too long so as not to choke out the other two sections of his life."

"So, what d'yu reckon they are?" Taffy queried.

"Taffy," I said "it's your home life and your recreation! Haven't you heard the saying 'All work and no play makes Jack a dull boy'?"

"Yeah, I have."

Swallowing my last piece of gunge butty and washing it down with strong tea, I continued "Well, it's true, if you work all day and half the night, you die rich and miserable. So what's the point?"

Silence for a minute, then Taffy suggested "You could leave all your money to the wife."

"Good grief, you know what would happen then?" I asked him.

"No, what?"

I laughed "She takes your money and goes off with another man!"

92

"Bloody hell," he said scratching his head "I never thought of that, I'm going to spend all my money from now on!"

Everybody had a good laugh.

Cowboy said "O.K., Taffy, we'll come round for a bevvy with you when we finish."

Taffy stopped chewing, glared at the Cowboy and said "Yeah, that's fine, can you lend me a fiver?"

Cowboy's brow furrowed "I thought you said that you were going to spend all your money?"

Taffy swilled the last of his tea "Ain't got none!" he said emphatically.

Billy chortled "You know what's wrong? Taffy's wife's got nearly all his money spent *before* he dies!"

"You're right there boyo!" Taffy declared, looking glum.

Cowboy turned to me "You'll have to come up with something else for Taffy, Haggis!"

"I've got the answer," Billy exclaimed "trade her in for a new model. One that takes less to run."

"Don't think so," Taffy asserted "takes a lot to keep up, but she's a comfortable model!"

That caused some amusement and with every peal of laughter Sammy was joining in just as heartily as the rest, whether he understood everything or not.

"O.K., boys," Cowboy bawled "back to the grind, we've been here long enough!" then swinging round to me, he said as he brought up wind "Haggis, I hope these butties of yours aren't repeaters!"

"That's their second name." I said with a laugh "They're called burper butties! They're a real bargain, you'll get the flavour all day!"

"Bloody hell, you might've warned me, Haggis." he moaned as he jumped out the wagon.

Billy and Taffy went on their way trucking out the full bins.

Cowboy addressed the lad "Jim, you and Haggis look after Sammy till Jack and I get back. If you get all the empties back, just wait by the first full ones. We'll be about half an hour."

"Where are you off to? Or shouldn't I ask?"

"We're flogging the slummy, it shouldn't take long!" he replied with a wink.

"O.K.," I said, and Cowboy jumped into the cab while Jack tried to sort out a few gears.

We walked back to where we broke off for tea-break.

"Where do they flog the scrap?" I asked Jim Lad as the three of us trotted along the streets to where the empties were.

"There's a scrap merchant on t'other side of the village, he gives us a good deal."

I laughed "It'll be worth it to get a bit more room in the cab. I'm getting fed up sitting on old lawnmowers!"

It took the three of us about twenty minutes to put back all the empty bins. When we caught up to the full ones we sat on a wall and waited for the wagon.

Jim Lad took the poem out of his pocket and started to go over it, trying to get it off by heart.

"You're going to make a great lover Jim, I can tell by the way you recite that poem. Some girl's going to lap that up."

"Yeah, it sounds great, Haggis. Reckon I'm in with a chance now!"

Just at that, the wagon trundled round the corner and drew to a halt by the first bins.

Jim and I tipped a few with Sammy and Cowboy, then fell back to return the empties.

We worked till quarter to twelve then Jim Lad shouted over "That's it Haggis. Let's get the wagon, it's time now for dinner."

When Jim and I got to the wagon everybody else was there, so when we were aboard, Jack engaged first gear with a mighty crash and with two or three leaps that would've left a young kangaroo standing, we were off!

Cowboy started to share out the slummy money. He gave some to Jack, some to Billy, and some to Taffy and Jim Lad. Then turning to me, he said "Looks as if you'll be with us for a while, Haggis, so you can have a couple of quid."

I took the money and thanked him, but noticed that Sammy didn't get any. I took one of my pounds and shoved it into his top pocket, giving him a wink as I did so.

His glum face broke into a smile and he looked over the moon. It was worth a quid to see the change it made.

We were trundling along the country stretch between Greasby and the yard when the engine began to shudder. With a final bang and a ph-ut, it gave up the ghost! The wagon ground to a halt as Jack applied the brakes.

"Bloody thing!" Cowboy bawled, kicking the side panel "Why does it always break down at dinner-time?"

"Flaming thing's clapped out! That's what's wrong." Billy ejaculated.

"Have we run out of fuel?" Jim Lad asked.

"Plenty of fuel," Jack retorted angrily "it's the engine, I've been waiting for this!"

"Alright, let's get organized!" Cowboy pronounced with an air of authority "Jack, you phone the yard and get them to send out the mechanics!" Then to Jim he announced "We'll have our dinner-break here!"

Jim wrinkled his nose and looked blank "How'll I boil the water?"

Cowboy rolled his eyes "Good grief Jim, put dry tea in the pot and follow Jack, and where he gets the phone, ask them kindly to fill the pot with boiling water."

"Where's the nearest place?" Jack asked.

"Halfway farm, we passed it a minute ago!" Cowboy replied, pointing back over his shoulder with his thumb.

Jack and Jim jumped out and ambled off.

"Let's have a picnic." I said, grabbing my butties and climbing out of the cab. Selecting a nice spot on the grass verge, I sat down to enjoy my lunch.

Cowboy leaned out the window "Good idea, Haggis" he said and he jumped down, followed by Taffy, Billy and Sammy.

We finished our butties and lay down to soak up the sun. After about ten minutes Taffy began to snore.

Opening my eyes, I looked up and noticed that an inquisitive cow had appeared and poked it's head over the hedge almost above Taffy. It seemed fascinated by the little Welshman. It sniffed then tried to lick his face, but couldn't quite make it. Frustrated at not being able to reach it's nice 'Welsh rarebit', it let out a loud Mm-ooooo not far from Taffy's ear. His reflexes were excellent. He shot up so suddenly that he almost banged the poor cow on the snout.

"Yipes!" he yelled and jumped back against the wagon. The cow got a bigger fright then he did. It went charging up the field at a fast rate of knots, scattering the rest of the herd.

We were all sitting bolt upright with all the commotion.

I looked at the stampeding herd of cattle, then at Taffy.

"You've done it now, Taffy!" I said "You've frightened those cows. They'll have blood in their milk tonight!"

"Bloody hell!" he exclaimed.

"No, bloody milk!" I countered.

"Give me the town anyday." he said with a sigh, wiping his brow and sitting down again.

Jack and Jim Lad came back from the farm.

"Mechanic's on his way." Jack said and went into the wagon to get his butties.

"Good." Cowboy said "Any bother getting hot water Jim?"

"Just a bit. He wasn't too keen, miserable swine!"

Cowboy laughed "Serves him right, then. His bloody milk'll be bloody tonight according to Haggis."

Jim looked puzzled "Say again!" he demanded, wrinkling his nose.

Cowboy explained about Taffy's experience with the cow, and Jim Lad almost burst his sides laughing. "They don't know what cows look like in Wales, it's all sheep they have down there!"

"England couldn't do without our Welsh lamb!" Taffy retorted with real feeling.

Just at that, the mechanic arrived from the yard. Stepping out the van, he sauntered over to Cowboy. "What's like the trouble?" he asked.

Cowboy gave him the standard glare "If we knew that, we probably wouldn't have needed you!" he replied in a voice to match the glare.

"That's true," retorted the mechanic "every man to his own trade. I'll stick to engines! You stick to your muck!"

GREASBY stretch (between NEWTON and FRANKBY).

The mechanic, whose name turned out to be Bill, climbed into the cab and removed the engine cowling. He banged and clattered for about half an hour. The cursings that came with every bang made even Cowboy wince.

Liquid started to trickle onto the ground below the engine. We all sat on the grass verge, enthralled at the sights and sounds of a mechanic at work!

Billy was sitting hugging his knees and looking intently at the stream of liquid coming from under the wagon. "What's he doing?" he asked.

Cowboy looked thoughtful "I think he's bleeding!"

Taffy scowled "Bloody hell, I wouldn't want a transfusion from him, look at the colour of it!"

Cowboy looked at him with disdain "It's fuel! He's bleeding the pump!"

"Oh!" Billy and Taffy said in unison.

Billy wasn't entirely sure "Is that what they mean when they say they've 'cut the engine!'?"

Cowboy's reply was to thump him over the head with his hat.

The starter growled and we all turned back to look at the wagon. The engine caught and slowly the revs mounted, and soon thick black smoke began to belch forth from the exhaust.

A cheer went up, then Bill, the mechanic thumped the engine cowling back into place, jumped down and gave a bow. He then began to wipe his hands on an old oily rag.

Billy was still curious. "What was wrong?" he asked the mechanic.

"If he told you, you wouldn't know any better!" the Cowboy interjected.

Bill finished wiping his hands "He's got a right to know." he said without any trace of a smile "It was the giggling pin that had come loose from the laughing shaft!"

Billy's face was a picture. He was mentally tossing up whether to believe him or not. The coin fell for the mechanic taking the mickey!

"Your giggling pin'll need repairing if I give you a kick up the bracket!" Billy exploded.

The mechanic looked at Cowboy with mock shock on his face.

"You've got a violent gang here, Cowboy" he said, "you should work them a bit harder to get rid of all that energy!"

Jack butted in and things cooled down "What's the engine like now?" he asked Bill "Is it alright again?"

"Yeah, it's fine now, one of the delivery valves in the fuel injection pump had stuck open. I've cleaned it out and bled the system. You should be alright now for another few years."

"That'll be right!" Jack spluttered, obviously not having the same confidence in the repair job as Bill.

"Thanks very much, Bill." said the Cowboy "It's good to be mobile again."

"That's O.K., all in a day's work." the mechanic said then jumped into his van and took off like a racing driver.

"Wagons roll, boys," shouted Cowboy, giving us the come on signal with his arm "your holiday's over."

We all clambered into the wagon. I was amazed at how nice and comfortable it was now that all the lawnmowers, scrap and extraneous junk had gone!

Our afternoon's work went smoothly with no problems and we finished in record time. Even with the breakdown we managed back to the yard for three o'clock.

I went straight home and had a meal, then I had a wash and shave and change of clothes ready to go back for the union meeting.

When I got back to the messroom it was just after four thirty and the meeting had started. Frank, the shop steward had the floor and was droning on "Yes, we've got a great fight on our hands. This crowd is ruining the country . . . "

The monotonous voice went on and on, almost sending me to sleep as I leaned against the messroom wall. All of a sudden he banged the table with his fist and shouted "Brothers, it's about time we got rid of this menace!"

There was a muttering of assent among the men, then Taffy shouted out "Do you mean Dennis, boyo?"

Frank glared at him, stabbed a finger in his direction and bellowed "No, but you're bloody close!"

Andy Cap thought that he would add to the levity that was beginning to creep in, so he held up his closed fist and roared "What we want is shorter beds and longer in them!"

There was a ripple of laughter, then somebody shouted out "Quiet!"

Instead of getting quieter, the hubbub grew louder.

Frank let out a groan which indicated that he knew he was beginning to lose control of the meeting. He banged on the table again and shouted "Brothers, brothers! Let's have some order. Before this meeting becomes a rabble, we'll now take the vote to see if we're all in agreement about withdrawing our labour . . . "

The vote was fairly close, but the majority were against strike action. That verdict didn't please Frank at all. His face was a picture of disappointment as he left the messroom. I went straight home, put on my slippers and had a nice quiet evening watching the box.

In the morning when I got to the yard there were only a few in the messroom.

"Have a good day yesterday, Jock?" asked the Bear without looking up.

I sat down and replied "Just normal."

"Not what I heard!" the Bear rumbled as his eyebrows began a tango "What, with a breakdown, an antique gate and a cattle stampede, I'd say it was abnormal!"

"Good Gordon Highlanders, are you in the K.G.B.?" I asked in amazement, wondering where he was getting his information.

Giving me a knowing smile, he replied "It's my job, Jock. I've got to know what's going on!"

"Alright," I said "what did I have on my butties yesterday?"

"Chopped egg and chives!" he replied as his eyebrows did a victory dance.

I was flabbergasted. I was beginning to be afraid of him. He seemed to be psychic and I didn't like it!

Cowboy walked in and sat down. The Bear said to him "You missed a bin yesterday."

"Which one was that?" Cowboy asked only half attentively as he started to leaf through his paper.

The Bear's eyes almost penetrated Cowboy's paper "Lady said that two of you fancied her gate but didn't fancy emptying her bin!"

"Bloody hell, did we miss it after all!" Cowboy said, slowly beginning to come to.

"Tell me the story!" sighed the Bear.

I butted in "It was just a misunderstanding! Cowboy said to Sammy 'Get that gate!' and he lifted the gate off it's hinges and threw it in the wagon!"

Another sigh from the Bear "Was it damaged?" he asked.

Cowboy replied "No, we got it in time. We were just putting it back when the lady came out."

The Bear scratched his head. "You'd better take somebody else today. Take Tom, it'll only be for a couple of days till Andy Cap comes back." Then swivelling round to face the old sweeper "O.K., Tom?"

"Sure." Tom replied and gave him the thumbs up.

Cowboy was stroking his chin "He can carry back with Jim Lad and Haggis can come tipping with me."

Old Tom looked apologetic. He glanced over at me "Sorry about that, Haggis."

"No problem, Tom." I assured him with a smile "I don't mind tipping."

The messroom gradually filled up. The Bear looked around, then announced "Looks like you're chewed up Cowboy, on your way."

The John Wayne drawl "Wagons roll, boys." got the gang to it's feet and we all clattered out.

I turned to Tom "We're breaking a record today, we're first gang out."

"Things'll move now I'm with you!" Tom said, laughing.

"No doubt about that." I remarked as we climbed into the wagon and roared off.

Taffy's eyes had a mischievous twinkle. "Thank goodness you're with us Tom," he said "you'll make up for some of the drawbacks we've got!"

"Such as?" Tom queried.

"Haggis for one!" came the quick reply.

I rose to the bait "At least I'm not afraid of a cow!" I said sarcastically.

Taffy looked pensive "The wife doesn't frighten me!" he said.

101

I laughed at that and said "Let's hope she doesn't Mm-ooo like that one yesterday!"

"No," he replied "but i was dreaming of her just when that happened, that's why I jumped."

"Is she Welsh?" I asked him.

"No, she's English. Born in West Kirby."

Tom frowned "Why didn't you marry a Welsh girl? I've met some crackers down there in my time."

"I like foreign models," Taffy replied with a grin "this one's built for comfort not for speed!"

"That means she's fat!" I remarked to Tom, then to Taffy "Isn't that right?"

He smirked "Delightfully plump, is how she expresses it."

A few more minutes banter and the wagon drew to a halt. I looked out and saw that we'd stopped at the gate Sammy had almost ruined.

"You get the bin, Haggis," Cowboy said "and tell her we're sorry."

"O.K., will do." I replied.

I jumped down and had a look at the gate before I walked up the path. The householder was standing by the back door. She laughed and said "Did you bring your camera?"

"No, I didn't. A photo wouldn't do it justice, I'll just remember it as it is. I'm sorry we forgot your bin yesterday, we're here for it now."

She was still laughing "A neighbour across the street saw all that happened yesterday and told me about it. Tell your friend with the hat that I'm grateful to him for saving my gate."

"O.K., I'll tell him, it was a near thing."

When I'd emptied the bin and brought it back, she was still there. She handed me a couple of quid saying "Put that in the kitty. You lot do a good job, you're not appreciated half enough."

"Thanks very much." I said, giving her a salaam and getting back into the wagon.

I gave the two pounds to Cowboy. He thought for a moment and said "We'll buy some cakes for tea-break with this."

Going back to our starting point, we all clambered out the wagon. Cowboy handed the two pounds to Jim Lad "Bring back some nice cakes for tea-break Jim."

"O.K.," he said and trotted off.

It seemed to be a well-to-do district we were working in. All the houses were either semis or fully detached. The big difference for us though, was that every house had about three or four bins and they were all quite heavy.

By the time tea-break came round I was glad of a rest. In a few minutes all the lads were back. Jim Lad scrambled in with a big bag of assorted cakes.

As we sat munching our cakes Tom said to everyone in general "Don't you think it's a bit affluent, eating cream cakes for morning tea in a bin wagon?"

"It's the district we're in, Tom." I replied "have you seen all the bins they have? It's a bit much, don't you think?"

He stopped chewing to answer "There's a simple reason for so many bins round here."

Taffy asked "What's that, Tom?"

"Affluence makes for effluence!" he replied, biting a lump from a big cake and spitting a hard currant out the window.

I laughed "Do you mean 'where there's muck there's money'?"

He swallowed the mouthful "That's right," he said "the more money that flows into a household, the more muck that flows out!"

"More muck should mean more tips!" expostulated Billy.

"Yes, I think we do a good service for the public, disposing of their rubbish!" Cowboy asserted as he threw some pieces of pastry crust out through the open window.

"It's amazing where they get all the rubbish." Taffy said, finishing his apple and throwing the core after Cowboy's bits and pieces.

A middle aged lady came up to the window, her face grim. "Excuse me," she said drily "I'm an environmentalist . . ."

Cowboy leaned out "Good grief, you don't look well. Have you seen a doctor about it?"

She was angry "You don't understand! I'm concerned about the neighbourhood. I saw you throwing food out the window!"

Cowboy was flummoxed, but old Tom wasn't. He smiled at her and said softly "Really, we're ornithologists at heart. We were feeding the birds."

She was more surprised now than angry. Looking at Tom with renewed interest, she said "You're an ornithologist! Do you specialise?"

"Yes," Tom replied "I like little tits."

Jim Lad was leering "I like big ones . . ."

"Shut up!" Cowboy barked at him.

"This is surprising," the lady remarked "I didn't realise that you liked wild life." ·

Jim Lad was grinning from ear to ear "Yes, we all like the wild life!" he growled.

"Will you be quiet!" Cowboy shouted at him.

The lady glared at Cowboy "Leave the boy alone." she said "it's nice to see one so young being interested in our little feathered friends."

"He's certainly interested in birds." Cowboy said as he held up a warning finger to Jim.

The lady smiled "It's been very nice meeting you, my eyes have been opened this morning. Keep up the good work. Goodbye and good luck." and with that, trotted off down the street.

Taffy pointed his thumb at Jim Lad "This boyo's going to get us hung if he doesn't watch what he says to the public!"

I sprang to Jim's defence "It wasn't his fault the last time we all nearly got the sack. You took his trousers off, didn't you?"

"That was only a lark!" Taffy argued.

"Yeah, we were all nearly larking on the dole!" Cowboy retorted "Let's get back to work, you've had long enough for tea-break."

. . . Old Tom was with us for two days until Andy Cap came back. Little did I know how long I was going to be on round three!

Chapter 9

ONCE A YEAR

When Rooster came back from holiday, Billy took his annual leave. By the middle of September, Taffy was the only one still to get his holidays.

On Friday morning the fourteenth of September I walked into the messroom as happy as a lark.

"Good morning all." I greeted the assembled throng.

"'morning, Haggis." came the chorus.

I thought I detected a flicker of a smile on the Bear's face, but put it down to imagination.

"Only two weeks to go Jim, then I'm back on the brush." I said, then I found the reason for the flicker.

"Wrong again, Jock!" he said with an assurance I didn't like.

I couldn't fathom what he was on about. "Taffy'll be back in two weeks, so there's no problem." I argued.

"There is a problem!" he exclaimed, waving a doctor's note in the air.

With a groan, I asked "Who's sick? Don't tell me it's a man from round three!"

"Right this time Jock." he replied "it's Andy Cap, he's got angina. So it'll be a long time before he's back, that is if he ever comes back!"

"Good Gordon Highlanders!" was all I could find to say.

He put the note back down on the desk. "Are you concerned about Andy or yourself, Jock?"

I felt hurt at the question. "I'm concerned for Andy of course, but what'll it mean for me?"

He grimaced and replied "It means that you're saddled with round three, or they're saddled with you! Whichever way you want to look at it!"

I brought up another sigh from my boots "So what you're saying is, that I'll be on round three until Andy comes back from sick leave?"

"Yes," he said tapping the note "but if the doctor says that he can't manage to lift bins, then he'll probably need a lighter job. If that happens you'll be permanently on round three! How does that bug you?"

Curling the end of my lip, I sneered "I'm delirious!"

"You can say that again!" came the usual Welsh voice from the corner.

I ignored his remark, as I was too busy thinking about getting worn out on round three.

Cowboy put his paper down. "What's the score this morning, Jim?"

Taffy piped up "Andy Cap sicks — Haggis nil!"

Cowboy gave him a withering look "Don't be bloody morbid," he growled "you'll be ill one day!"

"Sorry." the little Welshman said, casting his eyes back to the female form on page three.

The Bear's eyebrows were taking partners "Can I get a word in?" he growled.

Cowboy smiled "Go ahead Jim," he said, gesturing with his hand "the floor's yours, I just tidied it up a bit."

"Thanks very much." the inspector said sarcastically "You have yourself, Billy, Rooster and Jim Lad. Taffy goes on his annual leave tonight."

"That's right," verified the chargehand "so we'll need two replacements next week."

The tempo had slowed down to a foxtrot. That meant the Bear was thinking! The moustache took over "Skinny can take the place of Rooster for today, then he can do Taffy's stint for two weeks while he's on holiday. Haggis can now replace Andy Cap." He sat back pleased with his mental shuffling of the men.

Cowboy was pleased too "Fine." he said.

"On your way then!" commanded the Bear.

"Wagons roll, boys." Cowboy drawled in his best John Wayne take off.

Once we were ensconced in the wagon, Cowboy said "Looks as if you're a permanent fixture, Haggis."

I put on my best scowl and grunted "Yeah, looks like! Do you think I should be happy or sad?"

"Look at it this way," he replied "on here you'll get loads of work, big money and good friends on the gang. What more could you ask for?"

"Wah — wee!" I exclaimed "To think that I'll be spending the rest of my working life in close proximity to Taffy!"

Cowboy's laughter was loud and rich "Bloody hell, you two enjoy throwing words at each other."

"Yeah, but some of Taffy's are a bit spiked!"

"You hold your own though, don't you?"

I thought about that "Yes, and he does grow on you with time I must admit, but so does a wart!"

We looked at Taffy to see why he wasn't responding, but he was so engrossed in his paper that he was oblivious to his surroundings . . .

. . . In two weeks he came back from holiday, brown as a berry and looking fighting fit.

"Have a good holiday?" I asked him.

"Yeah, it was great, Haggis." he replied emphatically "I could live down there."

"Where's that?" I enquired.

"We had two weeks in a luxury log cabin in mid Wales." he said, and then went on to explain in detail about the log cabins; how beautiful they were and how the owner kept some unusual animals on his farm. There were beautiful country walks and river fishing. Then when he told me that dogs were welcome, I reached the drooling stage. There and then I made him write out the address for me so that Jane and I could go there next year. I sat back and mused over our dream holiday to come. . .

The threat of privatization of the cleansing department waxed and waned for weeks, leaving us puzzled as to what exactly was happening. Apart from that, the time passed more or less uneventfully until three weeks before Christmas.

On the first Monday in December, the messroom was almost full when I walked in. The Beak came in behind me and walked straight up to the Bear "Mister Carson," he said "I'd like to go on the bins for the next three weeks!"

The Bear looked at him for almost a full minute, which unnerved the Beak a little. "Beak," said the Bear as nice as ninepence "if a binman is sick today, or doesn't report in for any reason, you'll be the first sweeper to take his place. That's a promise!"

The changing expressions on the Beak's face were beautiful to watch. He broke into a smile. His face literally beamed. Ever so slowly the smile vanished. His eyes started to change, lids narrowing. His eyebrows came together, brow furrowing. Now he was scowling deeply. Realisation was beginning to dawn . . .

"B---!" he hissed, the word coming out like escaping steam "You know that no binmen'll go sick at Christmas time!"

The Bear kept quite calm as he gazed into the Beak's white and contorting face "If any binman doesn't report, you'll be the very first to take his place. That's the best I can do."

Without another word, the Beak turned on his heel and made for the door. I turned too and watched him go. Sure enough, he kicked it on his way out.

The Bear looked around as if nothing untoward had happened. "Well, well" he said "everybody seems to have the Christmas spirit. We're all here, so on your way! It's the first time we've had the three gangs all going out on time!"

We all clattered out, jumped into our respective wagons and convoyed out the gate.

When we were about five minutes out from the yard, Jim Lad drew a pile of envelopes from his pocket. He handed one to each of us.

Taffy peered at the one he'd been given "What is it? Is it a Christmas tip?" he asked.

"Open it and see." Jim Lad said, grinning like a Cheshire cat.

I opened my envelope and pulled out the card. I couldn't believe it! It was an invitation to Jim Lad's wedding!

"Good Gordon Highlanders! This is sudden, isn't it? I didn't even know that you were courting! Never mind, congratulations Jim." I said and shook him warmly by the hand.

Congratulations came thick and fast. Everyone shook his hand till his fingers tingled and his back was slapped till his teeth rattled.

"What about a stag night?" Cowboy asked, then added "Taffy's trying to get rid of his money, he'll stand a few rounds!"

"I'll pay my share," the Welshman replied "I'm not from Scotland!"

Rising to the bait as usual, I responded "For every round Taffy buys, I'll buy two!"

Cowboy was in good fettle "Bloody hell, Jim, we've got a good thing going for you here. Any advance on Haggis' offer? What about you, Billy?"

Billy was thoughtful "Look at it this way," he said "if Taffy buys a round, Haggis buys two, you get one, Rooster gets one and Jack gets one, that'll make six rounds. I won't be able to drink any more, so I won't need to buy any!"

"Miserable twat!" Cowboy cried out, taking off his hat and beating Billy over the head with it.

Jim Lad held Cowboy's arm "Let him be, he can have free ale that night on me."

"No way!" Cowboy barked "You don't buy anything that night, we'll supply the booze!"

The wagon drew up with a squeal of brakes. We had arrived at our starting point. I opened the door to get out, but the Cowboy put out his hand and stopped me "Hold it, Haggis." he said, then addressing everyone "Do we all know the score? It's the Christmas period, remember!"

"Yeah." came the chorus from everyone — except me, so I said "I'm not sure what you mean. Is it to do with the tips we'll be getting?"

He laughed "That's right, Haggis. We can't ask for tips, but we can chivy them up a bit!"

I was puzzled "How do we do that?" I asked.

"Simple," Cowboy replied "we announce our presence, make a noise with the bins and sing while you're doing it. If you see the householder, wish her a Merry Christmas and don't refuse to take anything, even garden rubbish!"

"I can't sing." I disclosed to Cowboy.

"Whistle!"

"Can't whistle!"

"Kick the bloody bins then!" he bellowed in exasperation.

"Alright," I said "I'll do my best, but who do I give the tips to? What's the procedure?"

He replied "Every time you come back to the wagon, give the tips you've collected to Jack. He'll hold everything, then we'll divvy up day before the holiday."

That week I collected over nine pounds. The following week I got about twenty pounds.

On Monday morning, four days before Christmas, as we were stopping to drop off the truckers Taffy and Billy, Cowboy said "This is the big one boys, pull out the stops and see what we can make!"

"O.K." Billy said as he and Taffy jumped down.

When they were out of sight, I said to Cowboy "I don't know how Billy's lasting, his feet seem to be sore. He was limping like nobody's business on Friday. Maybe it's those big wellies he's wearing."

Cowboy pointed a finger at his chest and proclaimed in a knowing voice "The Cowboy has found out his sickness! I'll cure his limp at tea-break!"

We started work and the going was good. Cowboy and I were tipping the bins and householders were tipping us!

At tea-break Cowboy, Rooster, Jim Lad and I were in the wagon with Jack, the driver. Jim Lad had just brought in the tea.

"Let's have a cup." Rooster said, holding out his mug to Jim.

Cowboy held up his hand "Don't pour out the tea till Billy and Taffy come back!"

Rooster was agitated "Bloody hell, come on" he moaned "we never wait for the truckers!"

Cowboy retorted "We do this time!"

Rooster's brow furrowed as he looked at Cowboy "Something's up, isn't it?"

"There is!"

I spied the truckers coming out of the next avenue "Here they come now." I announced.

Cowboy let them get almost up to the wagon before he cried "Everybody out the cab!"

"Hell's bells, what's going on!" asked the confused Rooster, but obediently jumping out with everyone else.

110

"What's up?" Billy queried when he came up and saw everyone getting out of the wagon. Hardly were the words out his mouth when Cowboy put an arm lock on him and threw him onto his back.

"Rooster, Jim! Help me hold him down!" Cowboy roared.

Billy was squirming and screaming "B---s!"

Once he was held fast, Cowboy roared again "Taffy, Haggis, pull off his wellies!"

I had his left welly off before Taffy could get hold of the other one. Holding it aloft, I turned it upside-down. Out poured pound coins, fifty pence pieces and an assortment of smaller coins. By this time Taffy had his right welly off. It held about ten pounds worth of various coins.

I couldn't believe it "Good Gordon Highlanders, no wonder he's been limping, the miserable thieving swine!"

The expletives came thick and fast from the gang.

"He's a b---!" the Cowboy exploded "that's the worst kind of thief, one that robs his mates!"

"Bloody pig, let's give him the boot!" Rooster said with hate in his voice.

"Hold it," Cowboy said, tapping his forehead with a finger "let's think about this."

He turned back to Billy. Holding him by the lapels, he snarled "We'll let you off on one condition!"

"What's that?" asked Billy from his prone position on the roadway.

Cowboy closed his fist and held it under his nose "You'll bring every penny back that you took over the last two weeks!"

The horizontal binman curled his lip "What if I don't?"

Cowboy's curled lip was more ferocious than Billy's "We'll beat you to a pulp!" he snarled — Billy brought the money back the next day.

On Thursday after work the kitty was shared out. We'd made over three hundred pounds between us.

Billy, Cowboy and the rest of the gang went to the Ship Inn that night. They were all bosom pals again and all agro was forgotten over a good few pints of best bitter.

The Christmas spirit in GREASBY.

I stopped at the off-licence, bought a bottle of sherry for Jane, got a couple of bones at the butchers for Blodwyn and Moira and two large pieces of frying steak for us, then went home . . .

. . .We started work again after the Christmas break on Tuesday morning. By quarter to eight round one and two were both short of a man.

The Bear looked round at the sweepers "Skinny, round one! Beak, round two!" then turning to our charge hand, he said "Cowboy, your crew's complete. On your way!"

We could hardly hear the "Wagons roll, boys" for the Beak shouting. He was screaming "Bloody f---- b----! If I can't get on the bins before Christmas, I'm not going on them now the tips are finished! — Where's the union rep . . .?"

We could still hear him roaring as we drove off.

"The Beak's angry." I said.

Rooster laughed "D'ye think?"

Cowboy was serious "He does have a point you know. The Bear should keep a record of how many days a sweeper is on the bins through the year and the bin gangs could put money in a Christmas box for them."

"That seems a good idea," I said "why don't you put it to the Bear and the shop steward?"

"Yes, I'll do that when we get back to the yard."

When we got to our starting point I was delegated to carry back with Jim Lad.

Once the wagon was well ahead of us, I said to him "The boys are all excited about your stag-night but I'm a bit more interested in your fiancée. Why did you keep it all such a secret?"

He laughed "No secret now, Haggis. We'd being going out together for six weeks and we suddenly decided that we were in love and made for each other. I asked her if she'd like to get hitched. She said yes immediately and we set the date right away."

"It's the first of Feb., isn't it?"

"Yeah."

"On the invite I see that her name's Rose. Why didn't you tell us about her, Jim?"

He wrinkled his nose "Didn't want to get ribbed by all you lot!"

"That's silly." I said "Anyhow, where did you meet her?"

"At a disco. When she told me her name was Rose, I knew it was an omen. We went out together and on the third night I read her Rabbie's poem about the rose."

"How'd she take it?"

"She's over the moon about it. Thinks it's so romantic. You were right, poetry does turn on the birds! You'll have to get me another one, Haggis."

"I'll do that, but tell me about her. What's she like? Is she nice?"

He looked at me in surprise "Bloody hell Haggis, of course she's nice! She's about the same height as me. Got mousy brown hair, grey eyes and she's always laughing. She's a real cracker!"

"That's great. What's her father do?"

"He's a postman."

"What's she do?"

"She works in an estate agents office."

I laughed "You'll be alright for a house then."

"Yeah, I might even get a mortgage at a bargain rate!"

"At the rate we're going we'll be all day getting these bins back. Let's get cracking!"

As I trotted up and down paths returning the empty bins, I thought of a nice wedding present for Jim Lad and Rose. I'd buy them a book of Burns' poems!

Chapter 10

PROMOTION

By the beginning of April everyone was thinking of the summer holidays again.

The first Monday of the month, I said to Jim Lad in the messroom "Where are you and the wife going on holiday?"

"Majorca." he said with a grin.

"You went there on your honeymoon, didn't you?"

"Yeah, it's great, Haggis!" he said emphatically "We liked it so much we're going back again. You going anywhere?"

I was just as enthusiastic "Taffy's put me onto something good. I'm taking Jane and the two dogs to a log cabin in mid Wales."

Taffy's eyes sprang up from page three at the mention of Wales "Going to God's country then, Haggis? You'd better keep an eye on your dogs though, the sheep'll go for them down there!"

I was trying to formulate a reply to that when Cowboy said "We're crewed up, Jim."

The Bear replied "What'you waiting for then? On your way." then stabbing his pen in my direction, said "Jock, I want to see you in my office as soon as the wagon comes in at dinner time!"

As I climbed into the wagon, my dazed mind was trying to think of what I'd done wrong.

When I'm in deep trouble, Taffy's on top of the world. As he settled into his seat, he chuckled and said to me "You'll have the office carpet worn out boyo, the number of times you've been on it!"

I ignored him and turning to Cowboy, I asked "Do you know anything about this?"

"Don't think so," Cowboy mused "the Bear said nothing to me. Have you upset anybody?"

Giving that a thought, I replied "Not that I know of, but on Friday I cut my hand on a bin so I gave it a kick. Nobody saw me though."

Taffy was still tittering "Be sure your sins'll find you out, Haggis!" he crowed.

When we got back to the yard at dinner-time, Cowboy said "Have your butties first Haggis, then you can go into the office and meet the Bear on a full belly!"

"Can't wait," I said "I'm going now!" then made my way to the Bear's office.

When I knocked on the door, the usual voice growled "Come in."

Opening the door, I strode into the office, eyes blazing and ready for battle.

The Bear motioned to a chair in front of his desk "Have a seat, Jock."

I sat!

He looked straight at me without even a blink, then his right eyebrow went up.

I glared back!

Like a bolt from the blue the question came "Would you like a promotion, Jock?"

It left me stunned. I tried to assimilate the question.

"Well?" the Bear asked a little impatiently.

No matter how I thought about it, I couldn't see any way a sweeper could be promoted except to binman and I was already on the bins. I wondered if he was having me on.

"Has the manager left, then?" I asked.

His eyes rolled upwards, eyebrows ready to cha-cha. "Hell's bells Jock," he barked "you'll have to climb over me to get into that chair!"

I was stumped "What's the promotion? I'm on the bins now, so what else is there?"

It looked as though there was a smile beneath the moustache "We're getting a mini-bin on Friday." he said, then waited for a few seconds before adding "Would you like to go on it?"

"What as?" I asked, still wary.

"Driver/labourer."

"What would it entail? Where'd I be working?" I enquired.

With a benevolent little smile he said "We're withdrawing the sweeper from Greasby. So, your job would be keeping Greasby clean, especially the shopping areas."

"That sounds easy enough," I said "especially with a mini-bin."

His eyes did another little roll upwards "You'll be expected to do some other things as well, you know!"

I was puzzled again "Such as?" I asked.

He started to relate the other jobs "You'll collect all the bins that are missed by the various crews. All the dead animals such as cats, dogs and foxes you'll pick up and any dumped rubbish as well. I'll give you a list every morning, then you'll go to Greasby and clean the shopping areas. When you've finished that, do all the missed bins and other extra jobs. Then you go back to Greasby and start your daily sweeping round. Every dinner-time you'll report to the office for any other jobs that have come in."

Trying as quickly to assess the ramifications of such a job, and thinking that it was all a bit much, I said "What'll I do in my spare time?"

"Very funny." he replied "I assure you that you won't have any spare time. I'll see to that! Do you think you're fit for it?"

I was still doing some hard thinking "What about wages and bonus?" I asked.

"About the same as you're on now."

"Good grief!" I lamented "you call that promotion!"

He looked peeved "Promotion doesn't always involve increase in salary. Think of the prestige."

"Driver/labourer!! Prestige!!" I cried, raising my voice to a higher key.

"Do you want it or not?" he asked huffily.

"O.K., I'll take it. A change is as good as a rest."

"Right," he said, smiling "the mini-bin'll be arriving on Friday. You can start on it Monday morning. By the way you'll have to work Saturday mornings overtime. Is that alright?"

"That's better," I said "at least there's something extra in it."

Going back into the messroom I sat down, opened my butties and started eating without a word.

All the gang were looking at me in expectation.

"I'm not on the telly you know!" I said as I chewed on a lump of corned beef.

"If you were, we'd switch off!" Taffy said, making a turning motion with his hand and adding "Click!"

Cowboy was agitated "Bloody hell, Haggis, let's have it. You got the sack or what?"

"I think the Bear's put him back on the brush!" was Billy's suggestion as he tried to guess at what had transpired in the office.

"Alright," I said "to put you out of your misery, I'll tell you. I've been promoted!"

"Told you he'd get the bloody manager's job!" proclaimed Taffy in a loud voice.

Cowboy looked bewildered "What do you mean?" he asked "What kind of promotion is it?"

I gave them the details of the mini-bin job and all the work that it entailed. Jim Lad didn't like the idea of me leaving the gang, but Taffy didn't seem to mind one little bit.

Cowboy's face was dark "Bloody hell's fire," he said "who are we going to get on the gang now?"

"What about the Beak or the yob?" I volunteered, giving him a big smile.

He wasn't pleased.

The rest of the week went by without incident. When we came back to the yard on Friday afternoon the mini-bin was in the garage, so I went to have a look at it. The Bear came in at my back "Like it, Jock?" he asked with a beaming smile.

"Looks good," I replied "but how long will it stay as clean as that?"

"That's your problem," growled the Bear "you'll get half an hour every day to wash it down. Every Wednesday night you can have two hours overtime to grease it, check it over and do some general maintenance."

"Hey, that's not so bad, that'll be four hours overtime in the week and four on Saturday!" I proclaimed jubilantly.

"Bloody hell," he said, tutting "always thinking about cash! Come into the office and I'll give you the keys and the log-book . . ."

118

On Monday morning I was at the yard early. It felt like I was starting a new job.

One by one the bin crews went out, leaving the sweepers and myself. The Bear dealt with me first "Jock, here's the cards for Greasby, there's eight, take them in turn. Just one extra job this morning. At the weekend there was a car crash on the roundabout as you go into the village. Clear up any glass or mess that's left, then carry on with your round. On your way!"

After checking the oil and water levels on the mini-bin, I drew over to the pump and filled up with diesel. Throwing on a brush and shovel, I headed for Greasby.

At the roundabout there was quite a lot of glass, pieces of trim and bits of red reflector. It took about twenty minutes to clear up the lot, then I went to the first shopping area. A shopkeeper spied the mini-bin as I drew to a halt. When I got out of the cab he was waiting for me, and he looked quite hostile.

He was a smallish, middle aged man and his voice rasped as he said "Going to get the place cleaned up at last, are we? We pay heavy rates and don't get much in return!"

That sort of talk rankled. 'Keep calm, Steve,' I thought 'remember old Tom's method.' Forcing myself to smile, I said to him "It does look a mess, but things are changing. The inspector has taken me off the bins especially for this job. I'll be here every morning to tidy up."

He looked me up and down "You a binman?" he asked.

"Yeah, that's right." I replied as I pulled the brush out from the back of the wagon.

"Good," he said "maybe you'll do better than those lazy street sweepers. Their silly little hand carts didn't help much either."

He stalked back into his shop and I got baled into all the litter lying around. Although it looked bad, it took less than half an hour to sweep the area and empty the litter-bins. Just as I was throwing the brush and shovel in the back, the shopkeeper came out again holding two full plastic bags.

"Can you take these?" he asked, holding them up.

Hesitating only for a second, I replied "Sure, anything to oblige a ratepayer."

"Bloody hell, things are changing." he laughed and threw the bags into the wagon and adding "Thanks."

I managed to do one more shopping area, then drove to the street sweepers bothy that the council provided in Greasby and started my tea-break.

The tea was still in motion from stirring in the sugar, when the door opened and in walked the Bear.

He stood and stared, then growled "You should change your name to tea-bag!"

"It's a worker's right!" I retorted indignantly.

"Wrong again, Jock! Tea-breaks are a concession, not a right. Unless of course, you want to book off and not get paid for breaks!"

"E-er-no, I think it's a good idea to leave tea-breaks as a concession." I said through a mouthful of corned beef butty.

A faint smile of victory crossed his face "Anyway, how far have you got?" he asked as he plonked himself down on a seat.

"Cleaned up the roundabout and tidied the two main shopping areas." I replied, wishing he'd go away and let me have my tea in peace.

He seemed pleased "Good," he said "when you finish your break, pick up Tom at Hoylake prom and clean the slipway at the lifeboat station."

I took a mouthful of tea and asked "Is it sand?"

He peered at my butties on the table and replied "No, it's seaweed and debris, there was a big tide last night. Some of the pieces of wood are too heavy for one man."

"O.K., we'll manage that alright, no problem." I said, then asked him "Would you like a cup of char?"

He looked round the bothy and said "*No thanks!*" then pulling a crumpled piece of paper from his pocket, he put it on the table and smoothed it out. "Here's two missed bins that have just come in, take Tom with you on those as well. The first one I checked on the way out and it's too heavy for one man to lift!"

"And the other one?" I queried.

"Don't know, I'll let you check that one. Empty it and see if you can find out why it was missed."

"O.K.," I said "will do."

He rose, made to go out then turned at the door "Still come back to the yard at dinner-time." he said and left, slamming the door as he went out.

I heard his van roar off with tyres squealing. It seemed to me that everyone who drove a vehicle for the council had a hankering to be a racing driver.

Finishing tea-break, I headed for the prom to pick up Tom. When I eventually found him, he had his arm in a litter-bin right up to his oxter.

Drawing the mini-bin up beside him, I leaned out the window and said "Lost an arm, Tom?"

He looked round and without taking his arm out the litter-bin, said "Haggis, what has no arms, no legs, but has four eyes and flies?"

I thought for a moment and replied "It must be a little winged creature from Mars."

"Wrong!" he cried, drawing his arm out and almost slapping my face with something most foul, then adding "Two extremely rotten fish!"

The putrefying fish didn't hit me but the smell did "Good grief, Tom." I spluttered, choking with the acrid odour "it boggles the mind what some people put into litter-bins! Throw them and the flies into the back of the mini-bin and come with me, we've got a job."

He dumped the fish in the back and the flies swarmed in after them. Smartly, I slammed the lid down to keep them and the smell suitably restrained.

Parking his hand cart well out of the way, we headed back along the prom to the lifeboat station slipway. We set to and removed all the debris. There were all sorts of seaweed, wood, plastic bottles and unidentifiable objects. When we had it all in, the mini-bin was practically full.

"Just room for these two missed bins." I said to Tom as I checked the addresses on the slip of paper that the Bear had given me.

We went to the first address, which was in West Kirby. When Tom lifted the bin lid, the back door of the house opened and a lady appeared.

"I know it's heavy," she said apologetically "your boss has already been. If you can take it this time, I'll watch that it doesn't get that way again."

"No problem." Tom said confidently, as he bent down and grasped the handle. He strained to lift it. "Oh," he croaked as his face took on a nice shade of puce "there might be a small one!"

"I told you it was heavy." the lady said, wringing her hands "Do you think you can manage?"

Tom straightened up "Of course we'll manage." he said, then pointing to me "Haggis here is from Scotland, he's tossed a few cabers in his time! He'll throw it in the wagon without even scratching his sporran!"

She looked at me as if she'd only just noticed that I was there. "What's a caber?" she asked with a quizzical expression on her face.

"It's a tree-trunk." I explained.

"Well I never! What a funny thing!" she exclaimed, looking at me as if I were a freak.

"Come on, Tom," I said "you lift one handle and I'll take t'other."

We just managed to lift it over to the wagon and with a few grunts and groans we got it up and over the edge, then tipped it in. When I took back the empty bin I was puffing a bit.

"Thanks very much." she said with a big grin on her face, then added "They must've been very small tree-trunks!"

I gave her a wan smile "The trouble is, I haven't been taking my porridge regularly. I'll have to go back onto it again."

She laughed as she went in and closed the door.

We climbed aboard the wagon and drove to the next address for the second missed bin. It was a nice detached bungalow and the bin was clearly visible at the side of the house. We both walked up the path, and I lifted the bin with one hand.

"It seems alright Tom, how did they miss this one?" I said, still holding the bin up.

"Put it down again, Haggis."

I put the bin down and Tom lifted the lid.

"That looks like the problem, it's full of garden rubbish!" he said, pointing to the greenery in the bin. "Binmen won't empty any bin that has garden stuff in it!"

"Don't I know it! I've worked on round three, remember. I'll tell the householder."

I knocked on the door and a beautiful young blonde opened it. My mouth dropped open and for a moment I forgot what I was there for.

She seemed to be well used to that sort of reaction. Giving me a big smile and showing a row of nice white teeth, she said "Well?"

"E-e-eh" I stammered "we've come to see about your bin."

Her smile faded "Yes, why didn't they empty it on Friday?"

By this time she had stepped out and we went round to where Tom was waiting beside the bin. As we approached, he lifted the lid and I pointed into it.

"It's full of garden rubbish!" I said emphatically.

She gazed at me steadily with her big blue eyes "Are you saying that the binmen refused to empty my bin because I put stuff from the garden in it?"

"That's right," I said, sounding a bit like Cowboy "it's against the rules!"

She smiled again and said "Would you two gentlemen like to come through into my garden?"

Tom and I looked at each other, but followed her through the door she'd opened in the side wall. My mouth dropped open yet again, this time in amazement. Tom's eyes went wide. It was the first time I'd seen him at a loss for words . . .

The whole garden had been flagged — no greenery in sight! All that was there was a fish pond, a children's swing and a chute.

"Good grief," I said, indicating all the concrete "where'd you get the garden rubbish?"

She looked at me intently with unblinking eyes and replied "At the greengrocers! We're all vegetarians in this house. Last week we bought more stuff than we could use, hence all the green veg in the bin. So what's your verdict?" Her voice rose an octave as she punched home her clincher question "Do we have to become meat eaters before you lot'll empty our bin?!"

"Lady," I said apologetically "I'm sorry, and I'll tender apologies for the binmen. We'll empty your bin now and I'll put it on my report for the inspector. He'll instruct the bin crew to empty your bin no matter what's in it."

"Thanks very much." she said and with a flounce went back indoors.

As we climbed into the mini-bin, Tom said "I've never come across anything like that before, Haggis. It really takes the biscuit!"

"We're always learning, Tom. Did you have a good look at her? She's a cracker. I wonder if it was the vegetables that gave her that figure?"

"Yeah," he said thoughtfully "but she'll probably eat some cheese as well!"

I laughed "Don't think so. Cheese is made from milk and that comes from a cow. Vegetarians won't eat anything that comes from an animal. At least, I don't think so."

"Ah well," he sighed "she can keep her celery and I'll stick to cheese!"

We stopped at the traffic lights "You're not still on red cheese?" I asked him as I got the green light to go.

"Yeah sure, it's my staple food."

"Good Gordon Highlanders! You're not a horse, are you?"

"Sta*p*le! Haggis, sta*p*le!" he said, accentuating the 'p'. "It's the main part of my food."

"One man's food is another man's poison." I said "Let's unload this lot at the tip, then we'll go back to the yard for dinner-break and you can have your red cheese bouncing butties. "

"Great." Tom said with a grin as he furiously puffed at his old pipe trying to kindle it into life.

We drove up to the tip and stopped at the office. Peter, the tip attendant came over and peered in the cab.

"Bloody hell, Haggis, what are you doing on that? Have you been demoted?"

"Actually no." I said, sticking my nose in the air "I've been *pro*-moted, it's a step up!"

He looked thoughtful "Tell you what, Haggis," he said "It looks as though you're on a good thing. Fill your buggy with fuel at the yard on Friday night and you can nip up to Glasgow for the week-end!"

"That would be fine," I said with a laugh "but I've got a wife and two dogs, remember."

"That's alright, take the two dogs in the cab with you, and your wife could sit in the back."

124

"Don't think the flies in there would like it."

"Ah well, just a thought. What's the company number of the moon-buggy?"

"C.88." I replied.

"O.K., keep to the left, you know where to go."

As I put it into gear and started to move off, he shouted "Bury Tom's pipe up there as well, this is a smokeless zone!"

We bumped our way up to the tip-head and unloaded, then came out and headed back to the yard.

As Tom was going into the messroom for his break, I said "I'll give you a lift back up the prom after dinner, Tom."

"O.K., Haggis." he replied, hurrying into the messroom as if he was desperate for his cheese buttie.

I walked up to the office to get the latest instructions from the Bear. He listened attentively while I related the story about the vegetarian lady and told him about the fully flagged garden.

"O.K.," he said "that's interesting. I'll tell Sam about it and get his crew to empty the bin every week no matter what it contains."

I grinned "Yes, how do they normally tell the difference between leaves from cabbages grown in the garden and those from the greengrocer?"

His moustache quivered "Don't try to be bloody smart Jock, I've enough problems without you!"

"Sorry." I said and wiped the smile off my face.

"Anyhow," he growled "there's only one extra. It's a ginger tom-cat."

"What's wrong with it?" I queried.

He looked at me in utter disbelief. "It's dead! Deceased! Lifeless!"

"How'd it die?"

He shook his head as if to clear it "Bloody hell Jock," he said in exasperation "if you want to carry out a post-mortem, you can, but when you've finished, throw it in the mini-bin and it'll get buried on the tip."

"Where is it?"

"On the Frankby stretch, just past Fairfield cottages on the left. It's lying on the grass under the hedge."

"Can I have another pair of gloves?"

"Yeah, I'll give you a chit for gloves and a gallon tin of disinfectant, keep it in the cab for jobs like that."

"O.K." I said, taking the chit, then going to the messroom for my dinner-break.

Tom was chewing his red cheese butty when I went in "Any other jobs?" he enquired.

"Just one that I can manage on my own." I replied.

"What is it?"

"A mortified moggy."

Taff's bereted head bobbed up "You'll be alright for meat to fill your butties for a few weeks then, Haggis!"

I opened one of my butties "Looks as if I've got a bit of it now."

Cowboy had stopped chewing. He looked slightly green. "Do you mind, you bloody gruesome pigs. Change the subject while I'm eating."

Taffy went back to reading his paper and I started on my delicious corned beef.

After dinner-break I gave Tom a lift back to where he had left his hand cart on the prom, then turned towards the Frankby stretch. When I arrived at Fairfield cottages it took me ten minutes to find the cat. It was a beautiful animal and there were no cuts or marks on it. Rigor mortis had set in though, and it was as stiff as a board. I threw it in the back and let my gloves drop in after it.

Just as I was closing the lid I noticed that it had a thin collar on, so I dragged it to the side and took it off.

'I'd better take that back to the office in case the owner wants it' I thought.

Carrying on to Greasby, I managed to sweep quite a few of the streets marked on the card for day one.

When I'd finished I went to the tip and unloaded, then made my way back to the yard.

I gave the mini-bin a good hose down — the first day on my new job was over!

Chapter 11

MISSING AND MISSED

On Tuesday morning the messroom was fairly full by the time I arrived. The buzz of conversation centred on privatization.

The Bear was sitting at the table, seemingly aloof from the argie-bargie that was going on. I went over and sat on a seat near him.

Catching his attention, I asked him "Where's this threat of privatization coming from, Jim?"

He looked at me pityingly and said "From the politicians, Jock!"

"Do you think they'll be able to do it?"

Rubbing his chin, he replied "Look at it this way. If they can convince the ratepayers that a private firm can do the job cheaper and allow the rates to be cut, they've got it sewn up!"

I sighed "Looks certain, then?"

Doodling on the sheet in front of him, he said "I'll give it six months!"

"Nothing much we can do about it." I said, half to myself, then opened up the paper to have a good read.

I got so engrossed in a story about a fight that had broken out at a top level peace conference that I wasn't conscious of the bin gangs going out . . .

"Are you going to sit there all day Jock?" roared the Bear.

With a start I looked up and saw that only the sweepers were left in the messroom.

"Eh-e-er, waiting for instructions." I stammered.

"Here they are then," he said, handing me a slip of paper "two missing, one missed."

Taking the slip, I glanced at it and saw that it contained three addresses. I mulled over it for a few seconds, then asked "Can you elucidate?"

He looked at me quizzically "Jock, how is it you can use a word like elucidate yet don't know simple words like missing and missed?"

I was huffed "I know what they mean alright," I replied "but I don't know how you're applying them to bins."

"It's simple, Jock." he said "The first two bins have gone missing! Lost! They haven't been returned to the house for some reason. You'll have to find them. The other one has been missed. The binmen didn't empty it, so you'll have to."

I said "Ah, I thought that's what you meant."

He put his head in his hands and said "Bloody hell, on your way Jock!"

Hurrying out the messroom, I got into the mini-bin and headed for Greasby. As I arrived at the first shopping area, the same shopkeeper that I'd met yesterday came out again.

"I don't believe this!" he said "Sweeping this area two days on the run! What are things coming to?"

Laughing, I replied "They were having a bit of difficulty, so they sent up to Scotland for me to come down and sort things out!"

"Well, keep it up." he said and vanished back into the shop.

It didn't take long to sweep the road and footpath in front of the shops and empty the litter-bins. When I'd almost got it finished, the shopkeeper re-appeared holding two bags of rubbish.

"Can you take this?" he asked, waving them at me.

Pointing to the mini-bin, I said "This isn't a bin wagon, you know! But I'll take it anyway."

"O.K., thanks." he said, throwing the bags in the back, then asked "Do you smoke?"

Thinking about that for a few seconds, I replied "No, but I do eat chocolate!"

He laughed and said "Bloody hell, you're not soft! Hold on a minute."

He went back into the shop and re-appeared holding a bar of chocolate "There y'are, chew on that."

"Thanks very much." I said, taking the chocolate "Just the kind I like, fruit and nut."

"Thank *you* very much. Will we see you tomorrow?"

"Certainly hope so!" I replied "And every weekday."

With that I got under way and cleaned one of the other shopping areas. Once that was completed I went to the bothy for tea-break.

I really enjoyed my break. What, with peace and quiet, a corned beef butty, one with chopped egg and chives, a bar of fruit and nut chocolate and two cups of tea, I nearly fell asleep as I sat with my feet up.

My conscience soon began to work. 'Better get going', I thought 'this is one of the reasons I got this job, the Bear reckoned that I could work without supervision!'

Jumping into the mini-bin I headed for the missed bin. As I turned into the main drag, I just noticed the Bear's van slipping past the shopping area.

"Crafty swine!" I exclaimed out loud "he's checking up!" and my ego took a little nose-dive . . .

The three addresses on the slip were all in West Kirby. I drove to the third one on the list. It was the one that they hadn't emptied for some reason.

It was a large metal bin with a brick sitting on the lid. Throwing the brick off, I tried to lift the bin. It was nailed to the ground, or it may as well've been, because it was so heavy I couldn't move it!

I knocked on the door and a middle aged lady opened it. She was on the smallish side, lightly built and wore glasses. She peered at me and said "Yes?"

"I'm here to see why your bin hasn't been emptied."

"That's silly!" she said, screwing up her nose.

"Why is it silly?" I asked her, feeling a bit silly myself.

She tilted her head back to look down her nose at me and said haughtily "Because I don't empty the bin, I only fill it. Ask the binmen why *they* didn't empty it!"

I scratched my head "Alright, but I've found the reason why they didn't do it."

"What reason did they give?" she queried.

"Would you like to come round to the bin and I'll show you why?" I said, and she stepped out and followed me to the bin.

Grasping the handle, I gave it a tug and said "Look, it's too heavy! I can't move it!"

She looked at me as if I was daft "It's obvious that you can't lift it. You're only one man, there are six or seven men with the bin wagon, aren't there?"

I didn't want to argue or try to explain how they worked the bin round, instead I said "What's in it to make it so heavy?"

"Just household stuff," she replied "and I've had a new fireplace fitted, so the old bricks obviously went in the bin."

With a sigh, I said "You shouldn't put bricks in the bin. Binmen are only human, you know. Even though they are strong, they do have their limitations."

"What will you do, then?" she asked, squinting at me.

"I'll empty it for you if I can get somebody to help me. Is there a man in the house? Your husband, son or anybody at all."

"There's only Jimmy and me." she replied.

"Alright, tell Jimmy to come out and we'll see if we can manage it between us."

In a quiet little voice she said "Jimmy's the budgie."

Desperately trying to suppress a laugh, I said "Don't you worry, go back into the house. I've got gloves, I'll fish out the bricks, empty the bin and then come and remove all your bricks as well. But you must promise not to put bricks in the bin again."

"No I won't, because I don't think I'll be needing any more fireplaces!" she said as she turned and toddled back into the house.

I took bricks and all sorts of stuff out the bin by hand until it was manageable, emptied it into the mini-bin, then came back for the rest. After sweeping her path, I put the brush and shovel back on the wagon and checked the next job on the list.

As I was pulling away from the kerb, the old girl was at the window waving. I waved back and could see Jimmy ambling along the window ledge.

Arriving at the next address, I knocked on the door. As soon as it opened, the lady proclaimed "I don't want any loft insulation or double glazing! Thank you!"

Laughing, I asked her "Do I look like a salesman?"

"No," she replied "come to think of it, you do look a bit scruffy. What is it you want?"

"Is your bin missing?"

"Yes it is! A binman took it out yesterday to empty it and I haven't seen it since!"

"Is it new?"

"It's a fairly new metal bin and has the number painted on the side and on the lid."

"Should be easy," I said "I'll have a look."

"Number's thirty six!" she cried as I went out the gate.

Going into the alleyway behind the houses, I checked in all the backyards that were open. Nothing resembling the missing bin was there. The only two doors that were locked were thirty four on one side and thirty nine on the other.

The number thirty nine was just discernible, so it seemed that it could be mistaken for thirty six. I decided to have a look over the wall. Walking up the alley, I found an old empty five gallon oil drum. I brought it back and stood on it. Lo and behold, in the backyard of thirty nine there were two bins, and one had thirty six painted on it.

I thought that it would be easier and quicker to jump over and retrieve it. As I was putting my leg over the other side, the fiercest looking dog I've ever seen came bounding from an outhouse. Barking and growling, it made a bee-line for my leg. Not keen on having my leg bitten, I didn't hang around! I made a leap for the alley! Jumping never was my strong point and this time it wasn't any different. I landed on my backside!

There I sat, in the middle of the jigger with a numb bum!

The noise had brought the householder out. I heard her shooing the dog in, then she opened the yard door.

She looked at me in shocked surprise and said "What are you doing, sitting there?"

Groaning, I croaked "It's a shaggy dog story and I'll tell you something else, with this new job of mine I'm thinking of extending my vocabulary to include stronger expletives!"

Giving me a baleful glare she grunted "What's your new job? Sitting in jiggers?"

Rubbing my painful posterior, I replied "That among other things."

Her brow furrowed "What other things?"

131

A numb bum in a WEST KIRBY jigger.

"Looking for lost bins! The lady at thirty six has lost hers and I think it's in your yard."

"Oh," she said "it could be, I leave the door open on bin day. They may've made a mistake. I'll have a look."

She went back in and returned with the offending bin. "Yes you're right," she said "here it is. Funny I didn't notice it before."

By this time I'd managed to get back onto my feet again.

"Thanks very much." I said and took the bin.

"Don't mention it." she said as she went in and closed the door.

I took the bin back to thirty six and the lady thanked me, adding "Where was it?"

"In thirty nine."

"Good gracious! What are binmen coming to? They're not the same breed these days!"

"Please don't mention breed," I replied "it reminds me of dogs!"

She looked at me in a strange manner as I walked out the gate rubbing my bottom.

Going up to the mini-bin, I eased myself into the cab. The next job was only three streets away, the address was thirty Hydro Avenue. It only took a few minutes to get there.

A large man answered my knock on the door.

"Good morning." I said cheerfully.

The response was gruff "What is it?"

"I've come to find your lost bin. Did you report that it wasn't returned after the binmen took it to empty it?"

His lip curled "That's right, they're a careless lot!"

I kept calm "No problem sir," I said "I'll find it for you. What type is it?"

"Black." he said curtly.

"Yes, but is it the ribbed type or one of the smooth ones?"

Glaring at me, he snarled "How do I know, I don't look at the bin all day!"

"That's not really important." I said, surprised at how cool I was keeping "Is the number on it?"

133

"Of course there's a number on it!" he rasped.

I smiled and said "That's easy sir, I'll go and find it. Your number is thirty." then giving him a wave, I walked down the path.

He shouted after me "That's not the number on the bin!"

Slowly I walked back up the path. "What number is on the bin?" I asked, trying to think how old Tom would have handled this situation.

"We got the bin from the Jones' who live in Mostyn Avenue." he replied.

I asked the obvious question "What's their number?"

"Don't know. I've forgotten." he muttered.

To say that I was getting slightly confused would certainly be an understatement, and I was beginning to lose my cool.

"How do you suggest then, that I identify your bin if I come across it?" I barked at him.

He was starting to get agitated "All you do," he growled "is to go to all the back yards till you find a bin with a number on it that doesn't correspond with the house number."

"If it's so easy, why didn't you do that?!"

"Because it's not my job!" he raved "Nor is it my fault, it's the fault of you stupid binmen!"

The hairs on the back of my neck began to bristle and a cutting retort formed on my tongue. 'Stay calm, Steve,' I thought 'remember old Tom's methods.' So I forced myself to say "It's obvious something has gone wrong, sir, I'll see if I can find it for you."

I went into the next backyard. There were two bins tucked in behind the outhouse. Lifting the first one, I looked for the number. It was so faded I could barely see it. I spat on the number and started to rub it with my finger to see if it would clear. Just at that moment the householder rushed out.

"What are you doing?" she roared at me as she stood, stern faced, her legs stiff and arms akimbo, like a female sergeant-major.

Putting the bin down, I replied "It's alright, I'm looking for a bin. I'm a binman."

My answer didn't placate her. "The bins have been emptied this week, so what's the problem?"

I sighed "Yes, I know. I'm looking for one that's been lost or taken back to the wrong house."

She tutted and said "It's not the one from number thirty again, is it?"

"Yes it is. Does it happen often?"

"All the time! You'll find it at number thirtythree across the way there." she said, pointing to a door on the other side of the jigger.

Beginning to get the picture, I said "Presumably then, the bin from number thirty has number thirtythree on it?"

"That's right," the sergeant-major replied "and Mrs Forbes is getting rather upset about it. She throws it out into the alley every week. She must've gone off for a couple of days or it would be out again."

"Thanks very much, you've been a great help, but could you help me just a little more? If I can get into Mrs. Forbes' yard and both the bins have thirtythree on them have you any idea how I could tell one from t'other?"

"Easy," she said "Mrs. Forbes' bin is a nice plastic one. Him back there! His is an old metal one!"

Thanking the lady very much, I went over to the door marked thirtythree. It was locked. Getting a bin from further up the jigger, I stood on it, climbed over the wall and retrieved the bin. I scraped the number thirtythree off it with my knife and returned it to the yard at thirty.

As I strolled back to the mini-bin I mused 'How about being a detective — Haggis, private eye — binfinder inc.!' . . .

Looking at my watch, I found that it was too late to go back to Greasby, yet it was too early to go to the yard for dinner., So I headed for the tip to unload, although the wagon wasn't quite full.

As I slowly went through the gate at the tip, I shouted to Peter "C88."

His cheery voice came floating back "Pass, moon-buggy! And don't be rooting at the tip-head, Haggis. The bosses are on the prowl!"

"O.K." I replied and made my way up to unload.

Going up the rutted track, I met Jack and Taffy in their wagon coming down. It was so tight, we almost touched as we passed.

Taffy stuck his head out the window and shouted "Move over and let the workers through, Haggis!"

I roared back "If you were a worker, you wouldn't be sitting there in the wagon. You'd be back in Greasby, working. You're a shirker, Taffy!"

The Welsh voice got fainter as the wagon trundled on it's way.

At the tip-head I unloaded, made a quick turn round and headed back to the yard at Hoylake.

There were quite a few in the messroom. Tom was sitting in a corner chewing on a butty. He gave a loud belch and thumped himself on the chest with his fist.

"You still on red cheese?" I asked him.

"Yeah, there's something giving me indigestion, but I don't think it's cheese or I would've had it years ago!"

"It's probably ruined your tum over the years, Tom. Why don't you try a good bit of Caerphilly? But don't let on to Taffy that I told you!"

"I'm here, Haggis!" came the Welsh voice from the far corner "Glad you recognise where all the good things come from!"

Tom gave another belch!

"That's what Tom thinks of you!" I retorted.

"If he'd stuck to Welsh lamb and Welsh cheese, he wouldn't have indigestion!" Taffy said adamantly.

"A good feed of Haggis and whisky would do the trick." I said, sitting down and getting stuck into my corned beef.

Taffy wasn't finished "That kind of stuff's O.K. if you keep a stomach pump handy." he said as he stuck a butty in his mouth, and I'm almost certain that it was red cheese he had in it.

When I'd finished, I went in to get my mid-day instructions from the Bear.

"Only one this time." he said, handing me a slip with an address on it. "It's in Hoylake as you see. She claims that it hasn't been emptied for two weeks. See what you can do with it."

I went straight to the address. The door to the yard was in the back jigger. Pressing the catch on the door, I pushed. It wouldn't budge, so obviously it was locked. It was a long way round to the front of the house, so I found a hole about two feet up the wall by the side of the door. Sticking my toe in it, I hoisted myself up, leaned over and pressed the catch on the inside. The door swung open inwards. I jumped down and went in. I closed the door, opened it and closed it again. "It's alright now!" I said to myself.

Opening the door again, I walked out and closed it . . .

I couldn't get back in! The door wouldn't open!

"Good Gordon Highlanders!" I muttered "It opens from the inside, but doesn't open from the outside!"

I climbed over the wall again and went up to the back door. A lady answered my knock.

"Good afternoon." I said, putting on my friendly voice "I'm here to empty your bin."

Her face went grim "About time! Why haven't the binmen been emptying it?"

Giving her a beaming smile I said "They can't get through your yard door!"

She moued her lips and exclaimed "Rubbish!"

"That's what they're trying to collect!" I retorted.

"Very funny!" she said, then asked as if she'd caught me out "How did you get through?"

"Climbed over!" I replied with a grin.

"Look here," she said and marching up to the door, pressed the catch and opened it wide "what's wrong with that?"

I laughed "Yes, but look at it from their angle, would you like to try the other side?"

We both stepped through the door and I drew it shut.

She glared at me "What are you trying to prove?"

I replied "Now pretend that you're a binman. Go in and empty your bin."

"Good grief," she grumbled "what's going on?" then stepping up to the door, pressed the catch and grunted "Oh dear, I can't budge it. What's wrong?"

"Well ma'am, that's why your bin hasn't been emptied, your door opens from the inside, but won't open from the jigger!"

She was beginning to panic "How am I going to get back in?" she croaked.

"Don't worry," I said consolingly "I'll climb over again and open the door from the inside."

When I'd scrambled over again, let her in and emptied the bin, she pressed a quid into my hand "Thanks very much," she said "I didn't realise, I'll get the catch fixed."

Giving her a smile, I said "O.K., and thank you very much."

Leaving another satisfied customer, I headed back to Greasby. Checking the card for the day, I found that I was well behind schedule because of the time taken hunting up missing and missed bins. To make up time I just sailed through all the streets that looked not too bad. Every really dirty one, I stopped and gave it a brush through.

While I was sweeping a channel in a very dirty street, and old gentleman came up to me.

"Good afternoon," he said in a refined voice "are you new here?"

I stoppd and rested my brush "I'm new to this job, yes, but I've been with the council a bit now. I've just come off the bins to do this."

He was quite a pleasant old bod, he smiled "Have you done Rigby Drive yet?"

"No, not yet, haven't had time to get round to it. I've been busy with bins."

"Oh," he said, looking puzzled "but you said that you came off the bins!"

I laughed "Yes I have, but my job is to sweep Greasby and do all the missed and missing bins as well as dumped rubbish etc."

He peered in the wagon "You and who else?" he queried.

"On my tod!"

"Oh," he said again "I see your problem, can I give you a tip?"

Grinning, I said "Yes, certainly, I'd appreciate that. I'm always a bit short."

He laughed "Not that sort of tip. What it is, I think you should sweep Rigby Drive as soon as you can!"

"Why, is it bad?"

"Yes, quite bad, but your problem is bigger than that. Some of the residents are putting round a petition because it hasn't been swept for three months and they're writing to the local M.P."

"Well, well," I said, scratching my chin "that is a good tip, I'd better go and do it now. By the way, where do you live?"

"Rigby Drive!" he replied with a smile.

"That figures, have you signed the petition?"

He shrugged "Yes, of course, what else could I do? When I saw you working hard I thought I'd better warn you. I don't like to see anyone getting into trouble."

"Thank you very much," I said, throwing my brush and shovel into the back of the mini-bin "I'll do it immediately."

He gave me a wave and walked off.

Hardly had I stepped into the cab and closed the door when a lady walked over. I wound down the window.

"Are you going now?" she asked.

"Yeah, I've got another job to do."

Her eyes went hard as she said "You haven't finished this street!"

"I know. I'll do it later, this other job is urgent."

Her lips were drawn tight as she hissed "If you don't sweep this street, I'll report you!"

"Dear me," I said "I wonder what Tom would do!"

She puckered her brow "Who's Tom?"

He's a psychiatrist friend of mine." I replied.

Giving me a funny look, she took a step back and said "Oh!"

I thought for a minute "Tell you what, I'll do this other job then I'll come straight back here and finish your street. If I don't come back today, then you can report me. Is that a deal? Shake on it." I said and proffered my hand.

She took one look at my dirty mitt, squawked "Eek!" turned on her heel and scampered off.

'I'll need to change my after-shave' I thought 'I'm not very popular around here!'

Entering Rigby Drive from the south end, I parked about the

middle. I stepped out the cab. Hardly had my feet touched the ground when a woman rushed over.

"Smell trouble, did you?" she asked in a falsetto voice. "How long have you been sweeping in Greasby?"

"Nearly two days."

"Two *days*?" she repeated, accentuating the word days.

"Yes," I replied with a smile "and Rigby Drive is high on my priority list!"

She was becoming suspicious "Who told you?" she asked, forgetting to speak so far back.

I was thinking fast "The Council didn't send me. I just want to do a good job up here in Greasby."

Her expression and accent were changing by the minute "That alters things somewhat!" she muttered in an angry and very disappointed tone. She could see her little petition game coming to an end without getting the pleasure of seeing it through.

I lifted my brush off the wagon and said "I'll have to get cracking now. If there's anything else you want me to do, just ask!"

She walked off, thoroughly confused.

When I'd completed the street, after knocking out all the weeds with the shovel and sweeping the channels till they were perfect, I stood and admired it. With some of the glares I got from the residents though, it seemed that they were angry that I had interfered in their fight with the council.

Loading on my brush and shovel, I headed back to the street that I'd only half finished. Polishing that one off in record time, I looked at my watch. It was now passed afternoon tea-break, nevertheless I took the risk and went to the Bothy.

Sitting down with a sigh, I poured out a cup of tea from my flask ..

The door opened and in walked the Bear.

"Good Gordon Highlanders!"

"Caught again, Jock!" he gloated.

"I've just come in." I pleaded.

He sighed "Don't panic, Jock! I saw you arrive!"

"Thank goodness for that. I had to finish a couple of very dirty streets and didn't notice the time."

"That's O.K." he said, then handed me the usual little slip of paper. "It's a missed bin, they want it emptied urgently. It's in Rigby Drive."

"You *must* be joking!" I exclaimed, putting heavy stress on must.

The right side of the Bear's moustache and his left eyebrow went up together.

"I fail to see any connection between a missed bin and a joke!" he said as his eyebrows waited to determine what the tempo was going to be.

"It's a long story, but I've just been in Rigby Drive and swept it from top to bottom!"

"That's funny." he said "Anyway, go up again, empty it and see what you can find out."

"O.K., I'll go up after break."

"Don't be sitting there all day!" he growled as he went out and closed the door.

As it closed, I stuck out my tongue.

It opened again suddenly and the Bear's head popped round "I can see through doors, Jock!" he growled and closed it again.

I went a shade paler. I was beginning to believe that he could.

After tea-break, I went straight back to Rigby Drive. Drawing up at the address on the slip, which was number fiftysix, I saw that it was about the place I'd parked the mini-bin earlier.

The house and garden looked very neat and tidy. Lifting the bin lid, I saw that it was only half full and light as a feather. As I was looking at it, the lady came out. It was the one who'd accosted me earlier, the one who spoke far back.

"Why don't you people do your job properly!" she said as if her mouth were full of marbles.

"Lady," I said "you're wasting council time and money, your bin's only half full!"

She started to lose her accent again as she shouted "It's not council money! It's ours, we pay your wages! We pay heavy rates to have our streets swept regularly and our bins emptied every week!"

"She's barmy." I said under my breath.

"What did you say?" she shrieked loudly, her aquired accent completely gone!

"I said it's a balmy day, too hot to work. I'll empty your bin. Any other problems, give me a shout. I'm at your service."

She went back indoors muttering.

I emptied her bin, swept another dirty street then headed for the tip.

Chapter 12

WHALE OF A TIME

By the time July came round, I was well settled into the mini-bin job. Doing it old Tom's way of ignoring the cards and sweeping the worst of the streets, I was able to cope with the extra jobs of missed and missing bins. The shopping areas I did every day, which pleased the shopkeepers.

One hot morning in July, when I got to the messroom there were only one or two seats left vacant. I stood against the wall by the toilet door.

The Bear looked up and squinted at me then looked down at his sheet of paper. After a few minutes he looked up again and growled "Bloody hell Jock, why don't you sit down? You're annoying me standing there!"

"No, it's alright, I don't want to." I replied "I'll be sitting all day!"

His eyebrows immediately went into a tango. Eyes boring into me, he bellowed "You what? I'll be watching you a bit closer from now on!"

The Beak, sitting by the window, said "Hell's bells Haggis, that's the wrong thing to say. You never tell him things like that!"

The inspector swivelled in his chair, and jabbing a finger in the Beak's direction, said "I'll be keeping my eye on you as well!"

The Beak's eyes rolled up "Now look what you've bloody done, Haggis."

I retorted "Pardon me for living!"

The Cowboy looked up from his paper and said with a grin "It's alright Haggis, you're excused."

The Bear gazed around, tapped on the table with his pen and said "I've got news for you boys."

Everyone stopped talking.

The inspector continued "I've heard on the grapevine that tenders have gone out to four private firms!"

A murmuring broke out among the men.

Cowboy spat out "Bloody hell, that's it then!"

Billy directed a question at the Bear "Why four?"

"They're the only four that they could find that are big enough to do the job. The council will put in a tender too, but if one of the private firms can do it a lot cheaper, then they'll get it!" replied the Bear.

That piece of news had livened things up a bit and the buzz of voices got louder.

While everyone was chunnering, the last three binmen had come in.

"I think I'll sit down now." I said, moving over to an empty seat.

"You're too late Jock, it's time to go! Everybody's crewed up. On your way!" growled the Bear.

The binmen all clattered out, leaving the messroom to the Bear and the sweepers.

He handed me a slip of paper. "Just one extra. It's a seal on the sand between Hoylake prom and West Kirby. The sand's firm enough to take the mini-bin. Do the shops in Greasby, then come back and pick up Tom to give you a hand with the seal."

Old Tom's eyes twinkled "We could sell it to a steakhouse, Haggis. It would make a change from beefsteaks!"

The Bear glared at us, and with moustache quivering, said "That would be a mistake! Don't leave it in the mini-bin, Jock, take it to the tip right away."

"O.K." I said, then Tom and I looked at each other, both wondering if the Bear had intented to make a funny or not. By the expression on his face you couldn't tell.

I said to Tom "I'll try to get back before tea-break, and we can have our break by the sea."

"O.K., Haggis," he replied "I'll see you by the sea, shore enough!"

The Bear was staring at us "Bloody hell, we've got the street sweepers goon show here!"

I gave Tom a wink as I went out the door. The mini-bin was ready to go as I'd checked the oil, water and fuel before going into the messroom to report. So I started up and headed for Greasby.

Twice on the way I had to stop and pick up things that had

dropped off lorries. One was a large piece of rope, the other an old torn tarpaulin.

It took only a few minutes to clean the first shopping area as the wind had blown all the papers and light stuff away. After emptying the litter-bins, I made my way to the other one. About half-way there I spotted a wooden box, obviously blown off a wagon. I stopped and threw it in the back.

"Excuse me." said a voice just as I was about to get back into the cab.

Turning towards the sound, I saw a lady leaning over the fence at the corner house.

"Excuse me," she said again "can I have a word?"

Walking over, I said "Of course you can. You can have half a dozen if you want, but it all depends, because my vocabulary isn't very extensive."

She was about sixty — sixty-five I would say at a guess and was laughing fit to burst.

"No," she giggled "I've had my fill of words in my lifetime. At the moment I've got a problem!"

"If your problem is a street needing swept, I can do that for you."

"No," she said, pointing behind her "It's not that, but do you see my garden?"

I had a look over the gate and replied "Yeah, it looks very big."

She nodded "Yes, being on the corner, I've got all that grass area at the front and all round the side."

"It's a lot," I said "but it looks nice and neat, you've obviously just cut it."

"I'm a pensioner and I can't do it but some lads did it for me." she said.

I now knew what her problem was, but waited for her to say it. Instead I said "It was very nice of the lads to do it for you."

Then she got to the point "It's left me with a dozen bags of grass cuttings and the binmen refuse to take them."

"Big bad binmen!" I said "But I've only got a mini-bin."

"I'll give you a fiver." she said with a smile.

"It's not the money!"

145

"What is it, then?"

"I'm afraid of the Bear!"

That stumped her. "I don't get the connection." she said, looking puzzled "Anyway I'm a pensioner, what'll I do?"

"Where are they?" I asked.

She pointed to the side entrance "Round there."

"Right," I said "I'll risk it. I'll drive round and load them on smartish, O.K."

Driving round to where she indicated, I threw on all her bags. Sixteen there were in all and they almost filled the wagon.

When all the bags were in, I said to her "There's an awful lot of grass there!"

"That's from two or three cuttings." she explained "The binmen never take them."

She stuck a fiver in my top pocket.

"I can't take that from a pensioner!" I said, taking it back out.

"Please," she said "my hubby got a good pension from his work, and I'm not badly off, so take it. I'm glad to get them away."

"O.K., thanks very much." I said, shoving the fiver further into my pocket.

She gave me a wave as I took off for the next shopping area. It didn't take long to do, so quickly throwing on the brush and shovel, I headed for the tip to get shot of these incriminating bags of grass!

As I was approaching the check point at the tip to book in, I saw that Peter was standing talking to someone — and that someone was none other than the Bear!!

I made to drive straight through and shout my number as I passed, but the Bear flagged me to stop.

He peered at me suspiciously "A bit early at the tip, Jock! What've you got on?" he growled, and as he was talking he slid up the side lid.

"Well, well, a load of bags!" he said triumphantly, tearing one open "How much did you make on this lot?" grass spilling out the bag that he'd ripped.

Glaring at him I said "You've got a suspicious mind. The binmen wouldn't take a pensioner's grass cuttings, so she begged me to take them, and being of a kindly disposition, I did!"

He pointed his thumb at the sixteen large plastic bags "An old age pensioner cut this lot! You think I'm daft, Jock?" he snarled.

"Honest! It was a pensioner! Young lads cut it for her!"

My strong assertion didn't entirely convince him. Still suspicious, he asked "Did any money change hands?"

"Really, Mister Carson," I exclaimed, putting on a shocked expression "do you think that I'd take money from an old age pensioner?"

He gazed at me steadily till I was nearly convinced that he was reading my mind.

"I don't know," he said, rubbing his chin "it's touch and go. Anyway, watch what you're doing! On your way, you're wasting good working time!"

With a sigh of relief I engaged the gears with a crash and shot up to the tip-head.

By the time I got to the prom at Hoylake, I was fairly late. Tom was sitting on a seat near the lifeboat station.

He looked at me quizzically when I drew up "Where've you been, Haggis? Did you go to Glasgow and back?"

"Wish I had." I replied with a laugh "No, I'd a tussle with a bear!"

Chortling, he asked "Who won?"

"Don't know really, I think it might've been a draw."

He yawned and stretched "Let's have our break here, Haggis. It's too nice to work."

"O.K., Tom, I do feel a bit peckish."

He drew out his butties and started chomping at the cheese. I started to unwrap mine, knowing quite well what was in them.

Through a mouthful of cheese, Tom said "Did you know that the Argentine economy is in a very stable condition, Haggis?"

"Yu'reckon?"

"Yeah, it must be," he replied "with all the corned beef you eat!"

I laughed "The cheese industry must be booming too."

Once we finished our butties, we sat for a few minutes, soaking up the sun.

Tom belched and popped something into his mouth.

"You still got a bad tum?" I queried "What was that you just took?"

"An indigestion tablet. They help quite a bit." he said as he screwed up his face and thumped his chest.

"You want to change your diet, Tom." I said "Tell you what, would you like to come round to our house on Saturday night for a meal and a couple of pints of home brew?"

With a smile he replied "I'd like that, Haggis. What time?"

"Six o'clock suit?"

"Yeah, fine."

"Right then," I said, throwing some crusts to the seagulls "let's go and find this sea-lion or whatever it is."

Tom clambered into the cab and commented "Yeah, the Bear says it's a seal, but I suppose he's only going by what he's been told over the phone."

We drove down the slipway and along the hard sand, heading towards West Kirby. Even at ten in the morning there were quite a few people on the beach.

Tom peered out through the front window "Where did the Bear say this thing was?"

I took a slip of paper from my pocket "It doesn't say exactly. Just says 'on beach somewhere between Hoylake and West Kirby.' "

Tom belched "That's a good three or four miles. It could be anywhere."

"Yeah, but it should be easy to spot" I said "there's not a lot on this stretch except a few rocks."

We drove along the sand all the way to West Kirby and saw no sight of a seal or anything remotely resembling a deceased aquatic mammal.

"What d'yu reckon, Tom?" I asked "Could it've been a hoax phone call?"

"No, don't think so. It must be here somewhere. Try going further out and we'll drive back slowly.

"O.K." I said and made a U turn.

Almost half-way back along the stretch we saw a kid just standing gazing at something.

Tom's brow furrowed "What's that boy staring at that rock for?" he said.

I veered the wagon over "Let's go and have a look."

We drove right up to the boy who hadn't moved an inch. He still kept staring at the top of the large lump.

The boy was on my side of the mini-bin when we stopped. As I was looking at the thing, Tom leaned over my shoulder had a peek at it and said "Oh!"

Turning round to look at him, I said "You thought that was the seal, didn't you?"

He looked disappointed "Yeah, I was positive."

The little boy was looking at a crab crawling across the top of a slimy rock.

"O.K.," I said "only one thing to do, we'll zig-zag from rock to rock till we find one that isn't!"

When we came to our sixth 'rock' it had blood on it.

Tom looked at it and remarked "You can't get blood out of a stone, Haggis!"

It was what we were looking for. Whether it was a seal or not, we couldn't say.

"Good Gordon Highlanders! Look at the size of it!" I cried out.

The head and tail were flat on the sand, that's why we couldn't identify it from a distance.

"It's big!" Tom said, stating the obvious.

"Yes, but do you think that you could manage it?" I asked him.

He looked at the dead animal, then back at me and said "If I had a little salt, vinegar and a few chips, I think that I might."

"Never mind trying to eat it, Tom. How are we going to get it into the mini-bin? Half a dozen men couldn't lift that thing!"

"Don't need any men, Haggis. We've got all the tools we need here."

"Don't be soft!" I retorted "all we've got in the mini-bin is a brush and shovel."

"Have you got a rope?"

"Yeah, but how can a rope help? There's still only the two of us."

149

Not too sure on the foreshore!!
Between WEST KIRBY and Red Rocks (HOYLAKE).

"Yeah, that's right," he replied "but we've got the mini-bin and it's empty, isn't it?"

"Yeah. So?"

"Right," he replied "what we'll do is, open the back doors and tie them back. Reverse the wagon up to the seal, then work the tipper to raise the body."

"O.K., what then?"

He was getting excited now. Gesticulating madly, he unfolded his plan "We tie the rope round it's tail, draw it tight and fasten the end to that tube on the top of the mini-bin. Lower the body and the seal will come up. Get some of that old wood that's lying around, put it under the seal and repeat the process till it's in."

"Good Gordon Highlanders, that sounds reasonable, Tom. I think I'll try to get you on here permanently."

Using Tom's method, we tied the rope round it's tail and hoisted the seal up using the tipper on the mini-bin till it was almost vertical.

It started to spin round slightly, so I said to Tom "You work the tipper control in the cab and I'll steady the seal."

Hardly had I got hold of the body of the animal when the rope suddenly slipped and the seal squelched back onto the wet sand. Only one thing different this time though — I was underneath the beast!!

I would've screamed but for the fact that all the air had been knocked out of my lungs.

Tom rushed round to the back of the mini-bin in a panic, shouting "Are you alright, Haggis?"

Once I got my breath back, I said "Yeah, I'm fine Tom. How are you?"

He was kneeling beside me, worried to death "Are you hurt Haggis?" he said, peering at my head and shoulders sticking out from under the sea-beast.

I spat out a mouthful of sand "Only my feelings, but I'd like to get out from under this thing. Can you pull it's tail, and I'll slide out?"

"O.K." he said, jumping up and grabbing the tail. He pulled and heaved. He huffed and he puffed, but it wouldn't budge! Finally, I said "Hold it! You're going to do yourself an injury. You'll need help."

Hardly were the words out my mouth when an elderly man came along. He took one look at us, then fled as if he'd seen an apparition.

"Bloody hell! What did he do that for?" Tom gasped.

"It's my after-shave. Never mind, get the shovel and see if you can dig me out."

He was back in half a minute "Can't find it, Haggis! It's not on the wagon!"

"Can you drive?"

He coughed and thumped his chest "Yeah, but it was a long time ago."

"Alright," I said "tie the rope to the mini-bin and the other end to the tail and pull it off.

Once he had the rope on, he jumped into the cab and shouted "Ready?"

"Go ahead." I shouted back.

It took him a few minutes to get the engine started, but when it roared into life he engaged first gear with a crash. Jamming the accelerator pedal to the floor-boards, he let the clutch out quickly.

The wagon moved about six inches. Not forward, but downwards as the violently spinning wheels sank into the sand!

I didn't see much of what was going on as the sand that had sprayed up from the wheels had almost covered my head and shoulders!

With my free hand I was scraping the sand from my face as Tom came round again, more worried looking than ever.

"Don't worry, Tom." I said, trying to console him "It was a good try."

"It's not that!" he blurted out.

"What is it then?"

"The flaming tide's coming in!"

I began to panic "Tom, Tom." I shouted "You'd better beat it and drum up some help!"

Just at that moment everything began to vibrate.

We looked at each other. "It's an earthquake!" I croaked.

Realisation dawned on Tom's face "It's the lifeboat!" he exclaimed in disbelief.

In Hoylake at low tide the sand stretches for about two miles before you get to the sea. The lifeboat therefore has to be towed out by a tractor. It had now arrived beside us! The man who had run away had called it out.

"It's a bloody walrus!" I heard the skipper say.

A couple of dozen people had followed the lifeboat out, so we were now surrounded by a sea of faces. I heard one little girl say with a giggle "It's a merman!"

Spitting our some more sand, I shouted over "Nobody'll ever believe a tale like that!"

It didn't take the lifeboatmen long to release me from the weight of the walrus. They even put it into the mini-bin for us and pulled the mini-bin out the hole we'd sunk into.

I was quite wet and a bit shaken, but I wasn't hurt in any way. We closed the rear doors and got into the cab.

There's a saying 'There's no show without Punch.' In this instance Punch was the Bear. As he hove into view, he roared "What the bloody hell have you done now, Jock?"

Coughing, I replied "Looks like I've caught a cold, a whale and a rollocking."

Once he'd stopped ranting and raving we set course for my house and some dry clothes.

Back in the cab again, I said "O.K., let's get cracking and go to heaven, Tom."

He gave me a pitying look "You alright, Haggis?"

"Yeah, fine. Why?" I replied.

"Where d'yu reckon heaven is?" he asked.

"The tip!" I answered without any trace of a smile.

His mouth opened like a fish "Haggis, how in heaven's name do you equate the tip with heaven?" he asked querulously.

I replied with a laugh "Well, every time I go up to the tip, Peter meets me at the gate!"

He laughed heartily "Good grief Haggis, for a minute I had a feeling that you were going bonkers!"

We drove up to the tip gate and Peter came over, twirling a bunch of keys on his finger.

Tom fell over on the seat laughing "I see what you mean." he chuckled.

Peter looked at him then turned to me "What's wrong with him? Has he had a whiff of laughing gas?" he said, then with his nose in the air, he sniffed and continued "I can smell it! What've you got in the back?"

"We've had a whale of a time on the beach!" I replied.

He slid the lid up and looked in "Bloody hell, how'd you get that thing in there?"

I laughed "My mate lifted it in."

He came round to Tom's side "Let me feel your muscles." he said as Tom flexed his biceps.

"Pass moon-buggy." Peter said, then walked away muttering "Some fishy stories we get up here!"

We went up to the tip-head and I backed the mini-bin onto the tipping area. Tom opened the back doors and I switched on the tipper. The body rose slowly and the seal, walrus or whatever it was, shot out with a splurge.

Tom's expression was sad "It's a shame," he said "this fella should've been buried at sea."

"C'mon Tom, let's get back for lunch. Which reminds me, I think I've got sardines on my butties today."

"Yu-uch!" he squawked, looking at me in disgust.

It wasn't sardines of course. It was the usual corned beef. By the time I'd swallowed three butties and washed them down with two cups of good thick tea from round three's black pot, I was thoroughly browned off with the chunnering about the coming privatization.

Wrapping up my remaining butty, I went to the office for my mid-day instructions.

When I went into the office, the Bear greeted me with "Ever think of going into the undertaking business, Jock?"

"No thanks!" I said, puckering my lips "Stiffs leave me cold."

The Bear was gleeful "I think you're in it now! You've got another body!"

"Good Gordon Highlanders! Two in one day! What is it this time?"

"A sheep."

"Sheep are heavy things. I'll probably need Tom again. Anyway, where is it?"

"On the beach again."

"Oh no!" I exclaimed "I hope it's easier than that one this morning!"

"It's only a sheep, Jock!"

"Yeah," I said "I've heard that word 'only' only too often! Anyway we didn't see it this morning."

"It's about half a mile up the other way, and you'd better do it right away, it's a health hazard. According to the report I got, it's been dead for a while and in a bad state."

Screwing up my nose, I asserted "I should get danger money for this sort of work!"

He glared at me "Don't be silly, Jock, plenty of people do this sort of thing."

"Such as?"

"Sewage workers, police, pathologists and the like."

Tapping my chest with my forefinger, I exclaimed "I don't get their sort of pay packet! Anyway can you give me a chit for gloves? A pair for me and a pair for Tom?"

He made out the chit and asked "How's your disinfectant?"

"Fine. It's about half full yet."

"O.K., there you are." he said, handing me the chit.

Going back into the messroom, I sat down and said to Tom "We've got another body."

"You could certainly do with one!" Taffy interjected as quick as a flash.

Never able to resist Taffy's inane witticisms, I responded in kind.

"When you snuff it, Taffy, Tom and I'll collect your body in the mini-bin!"

Tom was curious "What is it? And where is it, Haggis?" he asked.

155

"It's a sheep on the shore. I think it was trying to get away from Wales when it drowned."

Taffy wasn't beaten "Probably an English one trying to get to God's country!"

Tom turned towards him "Where's that?" he asked.

Taffy grinned "Ask Haggis, he likes to go on holiday down there."

I chalked up an imaginary mark in the air with my index finger and said "One up for Taffy. Let's go Tom, he's getting too good for me."

Tom and I got into the mini-bin and headed for the beach again. There was quite a crowd on the foreshore when we got there. Going down the slipway and zig-zagging through the people we eventually found the sheep. It didn't look much like a sheep any more! It had lost most of it's wool and the flesh had a greeny-yellow tinge!

"I don't like this one!" I said, screwing up my nose.

Tom was gazing at it. "You know, Haggis, I don't think even a self respecting maggot would go near that!"

Trying to gauge it's weight, I asked "D'yu think both of us could lift it into the mini-bin?"

"It might be possible. If you open the rear doors and back up to it, we'll give it a try."

"O.K." I said and manoeuvered the wagon into position.

"How d'yu think we should tackle it?" Tom queried.

I studied the carcass "You grab the front two legs and I'll take the back two. A couple of swings and it'll be in."

"Alright." Tom said, getting hold of the front legs.

I grabbed the other two.

"Right! Lift and swing!"

We lifted the dead sheep with difficulty and began to swing. Forward then back, forward again, then on the second backward swing it slipped through my wet gloves and the carcass landed back on the sand with a plonk! Straightening up, I looked at Tom. There he stood, gazing at the front leg that he held in his hand. He'd been holding onto it like grim death, but the sheep was so rotten, it didn't take much to part it from it's leg!

He held it up "Fancy a leg of lamb for your break, Haggis!"

"I think I'd rather be sick!" I said, and he knew I wasn't joking either.

"We'd better get somebody else. How about Skinny?" Tom suggested.

"What's he on?"

"Sweeping. I think it's round five, day two."

"O.K., I'll go and get him. You watch this thing doesn't run away."

"Alright," he said with a grin "if it makes a move, I'll give it a kick."

I laughed "You do that." and then closing the doors I went off to find Skinny.

When I brought him back, Tom was still standing guard by the sheep.

"Did it move?" I asked him as Skinny gawped at the sheep.

Before Tom could reply, Skinny, still staring at the rotting sheep, bawled "I'm bloody not touching that!"

"You don't need to touch it." I assured him "There's some extra gloves in the cab."

Tom, I and a very reluctant Skinny eventually got the sheep on board the mini-bin.

Winking at Tom, I said "Can't get three in the cab. Skinny, you'll have to ride in the back with the sheep!"

"Not bloody likely! I'll walk first!" Skinny bellowed.

"Only joking." I laughed "get in the cab and we'll take this to the tip, then we'll all go to the yard for a wash."

When we drew up at the tip gate, Peter came over "What've you got in the moon-buggy this time, Haggis?"

"Not a lot!" I replied.

He sniffed the air "Hell's bells, it stinks yet! You still haven't washed this wagon!" then sliding the side lid up, he poked his head in. Without another word he turned, put his hand over his mouth and ran back into the hut, face rapidly turning green.

"Haven't you ever seen a sheep before?" Skinny shouted after him.

"C.88" I called out to nobody in particular then drove up to the tip-head. We unloaded quickly and headed back to the yard.

The Bear was peering out the office window when we drove into the yard. He came out and hurried over.

"What are you three doing back in the yard at this time?" he barked.

"We needed Skinny as well to manage the sheep." I replied

He slid the lid up and leaned over the edge. When he drew back, his face was a picture. His eyebrows started a jig and his moustache quivered. Holding his nose, he croaked "Bloody hell, get this thing washed out!" and with that, ran back into the office.

Tom was laughing his head off. "D'yu think he'll enjoy his tea-break Haggis?"

"Probably not!" I replied "How's your indigestion, by the way?"

"Felt a little twinge of it when I was lifting the sheep." he said with a grimace.

"Yeah, the smell would put anybody off! You two get a wash and I'll hose the mini-bin out and give her a little bit of disinfectant."

They clambered out and I drove to the wash bay. When I'd hosed out the wagon and washed my hands, I took Skinny and Tom back to their respective jobs then headed back to Greasby.

When I reached the village it was almost time for tea-break, so I went straight to the bothy. For some reason I couldn't face my corned beef butty, so I just had a cup of tea and a biscuit.

After tea-break I looked around for the dirtiest of the streets on today's card. I found one that was really bad, so I parked the wagon and started to sweep it. I'd reached the last few yards when a man came over from a nearby house.

"Excuse me." he said "I've got a couple of kitchen chairs I want to get rid of. I'll pay you two quid if you can take them away for me."

"I'm sorry, it's against the rules." I said apologetically "We can't take payment for services. All we can accept is tips."

"Ah!" he said "I get it. Alright, if you take these chairs I'll give you a tip."

"Thank you very much sir." I said, touching my forelock "Just bring them out and I'll put them on the wagon."

He went in and returned with two old chairs. It was quite a struggle to squeeze them in, but I made it. Closing the lid, I turned to him in expectation.

"Thanks very much." he said with a big smile "Now the tip I'm giving you is a good one."

My smile was bigger than his!

He continued "Dancing Lady will win the four o'clock at Newmarket on Friday!"

"Yer wha?" I croaked, reverting to the local vernacular.

He was laughing his head off "Don't burst a gut." he said "here's a couple of quid as well."

I said "Ta." and watched him go back into the house as happy as old Larry. The little joke had certainly made his day.

"I've had enough!" I muttered to myself and throwing on the brush and shovel, headed for the tip.

Chapter 13

AUTUMN

Through the eyes of an artist, Autumn is the most delightful and beauteous of the seasons. Many other people in various walks of life enjoy and appreciate the changing patterns and beautiful colours of the trees and fields. Nevertheless to a street sweeper — it's a bane!!

To them it means leaves thick on the ground, wet slimy and rotting. They are the ones who are delegated the laborious task of getting them off the streets.

The time and motion people designated it unmeasured work, therefore not bonusable. So to the street sweeper Autumn is a season for more hard work and less money! Consequently that particular season is not popular with sweepers!

When I went into the messroom one morning early in October, the Bear was sitting in his usual seat, pen in hand and his roll-call sheet on the table in front of him. He had an extra item this morning though. It was a large pile of black plastic bags on the floor beside him.

I looked at the pile of bags and thought 'someone's going to be grafting today!'

"'morning all." I declared in greeting to the assembled throng.

There were a few acknowledging grunts from here and there.

The bear looked up from his sheet of paper "'morning Jock, windy last night, wasn't it?"

"Yeah," I replied "if I had a penny for every leaf that was blown down since yesterday, I'd be in Bermuda by now!"

Tersely the comment came back "Don't worry, you'll get your share of them today!"

Old Tom piped up "You should be on the prom, Haggis. Not a leaf to be had down there."

The Bear swiveled round to face the old sweeper, eyebrows getting ready for a slow foxtrot "That's true, I didn't see one single leaf, but your problem is just as bad!"

Tom took the pipe from his mouth and held it in his hand. "How come?" he queried.

Under the inspector's moustache a big grin was visible as he said "There's about two or three tons of seaweed been swept onto the prom with the high tide!"

Tom's smile had gone "Dear me," he lamented "I wish I'd taken my retirement last year."

Cowboy was taking it all in "Bet you wish you were still on the bins, Haggis."

"No fear!" I retorted "I like it on the mini-bin. It's like a holiday."

"We'll soon alter that!" growled the Bear.

Tom was laughing again "Haggis, you've got the greatest gift of saying the right thing at the wrong time."

With a sigh, I said "Never mind I'll survive."

The bin crews got their quota of men and went clattering out, leaving the sweepers to the mercy of the Bear.

His eyes slowly swept round the messroom. Everybody was watching his face, waiting for the moustache and eyebrows to go into motion.

They started when his eyes alighted on old Tom. "Tom, leave your hand cart in the yard, just take a brush and shovel. Brush the seaweed into piles, Jock can pick them up later."

"O.K., will do." acquiesced Tom.

The inspector's eyes were moving again, this time they came to rest on Skinny. "Skinny," he said "you take a good load of plasi bags and go to Springfield Avenue off the Frankby stretch."

Skinny was not pleased "Bloody hell," he wailed "it's about two miles long and lined with trees!"

The Bear was not perturbed "Don't worry, there's plenty of bags." Then his attention focused on me "Jock, drop Tom and Skinny off, then go on to Greasby. Do your shops and any streets that are piled with leaves. When you've done that, come back, help Tom on the prom and move the seaweed for him. Later on pick up Skinny's bags and take them to the tip."

"Good Gordon Highlanders! Is that all?" I said sarcastically.

He grinned as he handed me a slip of paper "No, here's two missed bins as well."

Skinny was still worried "What about dinner-time?"

The Bear was never stuck for an answer "Jock'll bring you into the yard for dinner."

He handed Skinny a pile of plastic bags and said "O.K., you three can go. On your way."

We put the brushes and shovels on the mini-bin and made tracks for the prom. We found the worst part at the north end. As we drew up, Skinny gawped at the seaweed "Bloody hell Tom, I'm glad I'm on leaves and not on this!"

Tom looked at the mess of seaweed "This lot would fill a good few bottles of iodine, don't you think?"

"Yeah," Skinny snickered "you could sell it to a farmersootical factory."

Tom laughed "Alright, Skinny, I'll put it in piles and you can have it."

"No thanks, you can keep it." he said as Tom climbed out the cab.

I started the engine again "See you later, Tom." I said as I engaged the gears and drove off.

When I dropped Skinny off with his bags, I decided to do the two missed bins in West Kirby before going on to Greasby.

The first one I went to, the curtains were still drawn. The gate to the back yard was locked. Putting my hand over, I tried the latch from the inside. It still wouldn't open, it was bolted near the bottom.

Nothing else for it, I rang the bell. It took about five minutes before a sleepy woman in curlers came to the door. She opened it a few inches and peering at me through bleary eyes said "Yes, what is it?"

With a smile I declared "I've come to empty your bin!"

"What! At this time in the morning!" she exclaimed sourly.

That extinguished my smile "It is eight thirty!" I asserted. "Anyway you should leave your bin accessible!"

"The gate was unlocked on bin day." she retorted angrily.

"Round two are running a day late this week, that's why they weren't here on the proper day."

"Oh." she said, stifling a yawn.

162

"Can you unlock the gate now and I'll empty your bin?"

"Alright, just a minute." she said, closing the door and going through to unlock the yard gate.

I emptied that one, did the other marked on the slip, then made my way to Greasby. As I was passing through Grange Mount a man flagged me down. When the wagon stopped, he came round to the cab window.

"Do you get many leaves on your job?" he asked with a grin.

"Occasionally." I answered warily.

He started to jingle coins in his pocket and said "It would be worth it if you could bring me some."

I hesitated, remembering what had happened on the bin wagon.

"Well?" he said.

"Oh," I replied "I was thinking about Cowboy."

He looked at me queerly "A bit old in the tooth for cowboys and indians, aren't you?"

"No, it's the other way round," I said with a laugh "but I'll risk it. I'll get you some. What's your number?"

"Fiftynine." he replied "I'll be here all day."

As I drove away he was still jingling his cash.

By the time I'd cleaned the shopping areas it was time for tea-break.

Break over, I jumped into the mini-bin and headed for the prom at Hoylake, going via Springfield Avenue to pick up the bags Skinny should have ready.

When I arrived at the place I'd dropped him, he was nowhere to be seen. He'd filled about twenty bags and left them in three piles on the verge. Loading them on quickly, I turned and made my way back to Grange Mount.

Drawing up at number fiftynine, I went in and knocked on the door. The money jingler answered.

"I've brought you twenty bags of leaves." I announced.

"That was quick." he said in surprise.

"Yeah," I said proudly "first class service on this wagon. Where d'yu want the bags?"

163

"Bring them round the back and I'll show you where to put them."

I carried in all the twenty bags while he stood and looked on.

'No wonder he's a fat little man' I thought 'he doesn't seem to bend his back very much.'

When I brought the last one in and put it down, I said "All present and correct sir. That's all the bags in now."

"That's great," he said "Thank you very much." then made to walk back into the house.

I was dumbfounded "Excuse me sir." I said.

He turned on the step "Yes?"

By now I was getting hot under the collar and it made me stammer "B-b-b-ut you said that it would be worth it to get these leaves!"

He grinned "It is!" he said "It certainly is! Saves me from buying compost. Thanks again."

The door slammed behind him and I was left steaming on the pathway.

"Blasted money jingler!" I shouted into the air "I shouldv'e listened to Cowboy!"

The mini-bin tyres screeched as I took off from fiftynine Grange Mount. When I got to the prom, I was still steaming.

Tom was sitting on a seat. Drawing up beside him, I said "You been sitting there since I left this morning?"

"No," he replied "just having a rest, got a bit of the old heartburn after tea-break. You look hot, have you been doing too much, Haggis?"

I looked at all the seaweed that he'd piled up. "Not half as much as you. Ease up a bit, Tom. You shouldn't be working so hard at your age. This is unmeasured work as well, you know!"

"No problem, Haggis. Don't worry about me. Have you heard the latest?"

"No, what about?"

Looking serious, he replied "A man passed earlier on and said he'd heard on the radio that one of the tenders for the cleansing department has been accepted!"

"Ah well," I said resignedly "the ball's on the slates this time! Did he get the firm's name?"

"Yeah, he said it's called 'Waste Away Limited.'"

"I've heard of it," I said with a laugh "it's supposed to be a thriving company. What d'yu think it'll mean for you and me, Tom?"

He thought about that for a minute "Well," he said "for me it'll be easy, I'll retire. For you though, it'll be touch and go. They'll probably take on a big proportion of the existing staff, so you might be lucky."

After mulling it over I said "Most likely take a few months to get off the ground so I'm not worrying about it. I'm a bit worried about your piles though!"

He chuckled "Do you mind, it's indigestion I've got, but you never know. This seat is cold on the bottom!"

"Piles of seaweed I was referring to. There's quite a lot, we'd better get mobile."

It took us about thirty minutes to load the mini-bin.

When the lids were closed, Tom said "You go to the tip and I'll put some more into piles while you're gone, Haggis."

"Not on your life Tom, jump into the cab. You're coming to the tip with me. The load could stick couldn't it?"

He laughed "O.K., Haggis, you win."

When we got to the tip, Peter rushed over. "What are you leaf-ing me, Haggis?"

"Wrong again," I chuckled as he slid the side lid up "it's weed you see!"

"Weed you see." he repeated "Bloody hell, seaweed! Are you sure you're in the right job, Haggis? Pass moon-buggy and don't come back, your jokes stink worse than the loads you bring!"

We did three loads of seaweed to the tip before it was time to pick up Skinny for dinner. He didn't look too happy when we got there. He had about another twenty or thirty bags in a heap on the grass verge.

"Hey, you've been busy." Tom said as he spied the bags.

Skinny drew his lips into a thin line and growled "That's nothing. I had more but some swine pinched about twenty bags while I was gone for a bottle of lemonade!"

"What!" Tom said in surprise.

I never turned a hair "I don't know what things are coming to when people pinch a few leaves."

Skinny was still growling "I've got a customer lined up for these leaves. He wants them for compost."

"You've got a problem." I told him "How are you going to deliver them?"

"That's your part, Haggis. If you deliver the leaves to him in the mini-bin I'll give you a quid from the tip."

· "A quid?"

"Yeah, I've done all the work, don't forget!"

"Alright, as long as it's not too far away and the Bear doesn't see us."

"Can you come at half three? I'll have them all ready by then."

"O.K., hop in, it's about time we were going back for our dinner."

We had our dinner-break, then the three of us got in the cab and I ran Skinny back to Springfield Avenue first, then went back to the prom with Tom.

Three more loads to the tip then we had afternoon tea-break in the cab with the flasks we'd filled at lunch time.

After break, one more load cleared all the seaweed. We took it to the tip, then went to Springfield Avenue to pick up Skinny and his leaves. We crammed all the full plastic bags into the mini-bin and took them to the address that Skinny had given me.

The old fellow gave him three quid. He gave me one saying "There y'are Haggis, that's the delivery fee."

When we got back to the yard at finishing time, I overheard the Bear say to Skinny "I've been to Springfield Avenue and you've done a grand job up there, lad. I didn't think you had it in you."

Skinny was a picture of innocence "I always do my work well Mister Carson, it pays in the long run."

The hairy foxtrot was starting. The Bear was thinking, and by the look on his face he'd just cottoned on to why Skinny had worked so hard. He growled "And in the bloody short run too, I'll bet!"

When I went home that night, I was shattered. There was no one in the house when I went in. Jane had gone out walking the dogs and by the time she got back I'd fallen fast asleep in the chair. She gave the chair a kick "Wake up lazy bones, night-time's for sleeping."

166

Waking up with a start, I rubbed my eyes and moaned "Can't you let a man rest?"

She glared at me balefully "This mini-bin's taking more out of you than the bins ever did."

"Yeah, it's getting a bit much." I muttered wearily.

Her little mind was ticking over. Suddenly her face lit up as she thought of something "Why don't you ask that inspector fellow for another man to help you?"

"Hey, that's a good idea. I never thought of that. I'll see him in the morning."

"Are you taking me out tonight?" she asked in her very best wheedling voice.

"I've got a headache!"

"That's my line!"

"Yeah, but this is man's lib!"

She scowled and gave the chair another kick.

I capitulated "O.K., the Country Club."

Her expression changed "Alright honeybun, you get a wash and I'll pour us a small one for starters . . ."

. . .Once the bin gangs had gone out in the morning, I said to the Bear "It's getting a bit heavy on the mini-bin, Jim. I could do with another man."

The foxtrot came, then the words "I'll think about it. See me at dinner-time."

"O.K., thanks."

The morning wasn't too bad. Just two missed bins, all the shopping areas at Greasby, some bad streets and Skinny's bags of leaves.

When I'd consumed my butties at lunch time, I went in to see the Bear.

When he saw me he said "You can have your man, but you'll have a couple of extras."

"Who's the man?"

"Tom."

"Good. And the extras?"

167

"Well, if I take Tom off the prom, you'll have to clear the litter bins along there every morning."

"That's fine, but you said a couple?"

"Yeah," he replied, as his moustache quivered "round three are slipping behind, you'll have to do the farm bins for them."

"Good Gordon Highlanders! How many are there?"

"Eight all told."

"O.K., if I've got Tom it'll be half the battle."

Tom and I worked out a nice schedule for all the work we had to do. So October slipped past with no more problems.

The
Binmen
are

Coming

Chapter 14

DEATH KNELL

One morning early in November the Bear was giving Tom and me our instructions "Here y'are Jock," he said, handing me the usual slip of paper "one missed bin in Hoylake, one dead fox in a lady's garden in West Kirby and the first six baskets on the prom are chock-a-block."

Tom and I looked at him in astonishment. I left it to Tom, who said "Can't be, Jim. There's hardly anyone on the prom these days, it's winter and it's perishing."

The Bear's face was a picture, utter amazement that anyone would challenge his statement. I watched his moustache and eyebrows. I'm sure the three of them were trying a square dance. He glared at Tom. "Do you think I'm going blind or senile?" he growled.

Tom was put off a little "Well no, not really Jim, but . . ."

"No buts," barked the Bear "do the prom first, then carry on with your usual round. On your way!"

We decided the best thing to do was to get out quickly before he exploded. Climbing aboard the mini-bin we made for the prom.

Driving down the road leading onto the prom, we turned the corner and stopped.

"What d'yu reckon, Tom?"

He stared along the prom, took his cap off and scratched his head. "Can't believe it." he said in surprise "it looks as though the first half dozen baskets are full!"

I laughed "You can't beat the Bear, can you?"

"No," sighed Tom "he probably makes a tour of the whole district before he comes into the yard in the morning."

"Never mind," I said "let's have a look." and drove up to the first one.

The bin was on Tom's side "It's newspapers." he said.

We both got out and rummaged through the papers. They were all the same.

"Tom, you know what this is. It's one of the free papers that's delivered each week."

"Bloody lazy swines!" he exclaimed "It's the distributors. They're paid to deliver them and they just dump them in here instead!"

"I've never seen them before. In the bins, I mean."

"Yeah, probably a one off, let's throw them all in the wagon and we can tell the Bear about it."

We emptied all the baskets and litter-bins on the prom, did the missed bin in Hoylake, then headed for the next job which was the dead fox.

The house was on the outskirts of West Kirby. We found it and drove in the wide driveway. There was nothing to be seen at the front.

We parked the wagon and got out the cab. The large lawn was clear.

"Must be round the back, Tom."

Just at that point, a woman came out and called over "Is it the fox?"

Tom replied "That's right, where is it?"

She pointed to the side of the house and said "Just under those trees."

We walked over to where she'd indicated and there, lying among the dead leaves was the poor old fox.

Tom was standing still, gazing at it. "Wonder how he died, Haggis?"

"Don't know, but he's not in a very good state, is he?"

Before he could say anything, the lady who'd came up behind us said "My boy wants the tail."

I didn't like the sound of that "What for?" I asked her.

"There's five or ten pounds on a fox's tail." she replied.

Tom saw that I was getting angry. "Steady, Haggis." he cautioned.

I ignored his warning "If your boy wants the tail, he can flaming cut it off himself!" I shouted at her "Why didn't he do it before!"

"Hold that bag, Tom." I said, giving him the plastic bag I'd brought with me.

We put the dead fox in the bag, threw it in the mini-bin and drove off, leaving her standing there, fuming.

"She just might report you, Haggis."

"Don't care." I replied "Don't like her type, with her big house and all she's got, she still wants a fiver for a fox's tail!"

Tom puffed at his old pipe, trying to get it going and in between puffs, said "Takes all kinds, Haggis!"

We went to Greasby and managed one shopping area before tea-break.

I had corned beef butties and two cups of tea. Tom had a cheese butty, a sausage roll, two cups of tea and two large indigestion tablets.

I watched him grueing as he tried to swallow the tablets. "How's that indigestion of yours?" I asked him.

"Well, let's put it this way," he replied as he thumped his chest "it's not going away. These tablets don't seem to help much."

Swallowing my last drop of tea, I said "Don't you think you should go to the doctor?"

He looked vexed "For indigestion? Don't be daft!"

"Listen Tom, he could give you some decent medicine. Maybe some good advice as well. I'd try it if I were you."

He took out his pipe and stoked it up with tobacco "Yeah, I might at that. Today's Wednesday, I'll take a day off on Monday and go then."

I sighed "Tom, why don't you go tonight?"

"What's the rush? You getting commission?"

"Never put off till tomorrow what you can do today! That's the saying."

"Yes, that might be true, but didn't you know that nature, time and patience are the three great physicians?"

"Procrastination is the thief of time, Tom!"

"Patience is a virtue, Haggis!"

Laughing, I said "I don't think anyone's going to win this proverbial argument."

"Yeah, we'd better get cracking, we've a lot to do." he said as he extinguished his pipe.

We did a good day's work and we were both going home tired and hungry. When Tom was going out the gate at stopping time, I still had half an hour to do, washing down the mini-bin.

"See you in the morning Tom, sleep well."

He gave me a wave "Thanks Haggis, I won't need a sleeping pill tonight! See you tomorrow."

I washed the wagon and went home . . .

The following morning the weather was fine again and I arrived at the yard full of beans and the joie de vivre. I was whistling as I approached the messroom.

'Must be the first here' I thought 'can't hear any chatter from the men.' You could usually hear the din halfway down the yard.

When I opened the door and walked in, I found the messroom nearly full — but dead quiet.

"Good Gordon Highlanders! This place is like a morgue!"

The silence seemed to deepen.

Lowering my voice, I whispered "What's wrong?"

The Bear lifted his eyes from the paper in front of him. His eyebrows were motionless, not even his moustache moved as he said quietly "Tom's dead!"

Two words and I couldn't accept them — just couldn't absorb the statement.

With a catch in my voice, I muttered "He can't be dead, there was nothing wrong. All he had was a bit of indigestion."

"Jock, it wasn't indigestion. It was his heart, he died of a heart attack early last night."

It still wouldn't go in. I couldn't believe it. All I could say was "Tom — dead!"

The Bear did his best "He was sixty-five, Jock. He had a good innings."

"Good grief! Sixty-five! That isn't much . . ."

The words dried up and my eyes were getting wet, so I walked out the messroom.

Sitting on the low wall outside I thought about Tom, his red cheese, the sheep, the seal and his kindly approach to life. Now he was dead! Why couldn't it've been somebody else? Somebody like Taffy . . .

The messroom door opened. Taffy came out and walked across to where I was sitting.

"Boyo," he said "I'm really sorry about Tom, I know how close you two were."

As I watched him walk away, I couldn't help thinking that a minute ago I was wishing him dead. He surprised me with his unexpected sympathy and I found my animosity towards him diminishing.

The Bear came out and handed me a slip. "There y'are Jock, two missed bins in West Kirby, do them on your way to Greasby."

"O.K., thanks. By the way, who've I got?"

"Take Skinny. That alright?"

"Yeah, that's fine." and turning to Skinny, who'd walked out the messroom behind the Bear "C'mon Skinny, let's go."

All he could talk about was the coming take-over by the private firm.

"It'll make no difference to you." I assured him.

"We'll be made redundant!" he kept saying.

"Skinny, the new firm will take you on no problem, you're young. The only difference will be that the wagons'll be a new colour and have another name on the side. You might even get a rise!"

That seemed to pacify him and he didn't natter so much about the coming redundancies.

We did our day's work alright, but it wasn't the same. Tom's psychology and humour were missing and I kept thinking about him.

When we'd finished and I was hosing down the mini-bin on the wash bay the Bear came over.

"Jock, the funeral's on Monday."

I turned off the water "What time?"

"One-thirty at Frankby cemetery."

"Can I have time off?"

"Sure." he replied "If you tidy yourself up at dinner-time, you can take the mini-bin. Park it well away from the cemetery somewhere and walk the rest. That O.K.?"

173

"Thanks. Any of the others going?"

"Anybody that wants to can go as long as they catch up with their work." the Bear said, which I reckon was fair enough.

Monday dinner-time I had a wash, put on a tie and clean jacket that I'd brought with me, then made my way to the cemetery. Skinny didn't want to go so I left him at the yard.

When I arrived there was nobody around. Spotting a cemetery worker, I asked him where the one-thirty burial was to be. He pointed to a newly dug grave.

"Thanks very much." I said and waited under a tree where I could see everything.

The service at the church was quite short so I didn't have long to wait. The cortege came in through the gate and moved slowly towards the graveside. The cortege consisted of the hearse and one car from the funeral parlour followed by one private car. A crowd of binmen walked behind.

When the hearse stopped near the grave, I went over to get a better view. They brought the coffin over and placed it on the boards, then the padre said a few words. As he finished, the funeral director picked up the first cord and called over to a man to take the end. He turned out to be Tom's only brother from down south.

The director picked up the second cord and looked at us standing by.

"Would some of his workmates like to take the other cords?" he said.

"Yes." I replied quickly and went over and took the cord. The binmen took the others.

"Lift." called the director once we'd all grasped a cord each. As we took the weight of the coffin, I saw the padre lift a handful of earth.

"Lower slowly." the director's voice continued.

When we'd eased the coffin into the grave and dropped the cords in after it, the padre's voice took over "Dust to dust, ashes to ashes . . ."

I wasn't listening. Instead, I thought that I could hear Tom's voice ". . . Haggis, if you eat plenty of cheese and use psychology, you can't lose . . ."

I stumbled back onto the grass.

A hand steadied me "You alright, Haggis?" — it was Taffy's voice.

"Yeah." I murmured.

He continued "It'll be about five before we're finished our round now. Would you like to come for a pint when we get back from Greasby tonight?"

"Sure Taffy, that would be fine. I'll meet you at the yard when you finish."

"O.K." he said and made his way down with the rest of the gang.

From that point on, Taffy and I became the best of friends. It was a great pity that it had to take something like this to make Taffy and me buddies.

The next few weeks dragged by and news that the take-over by the private firm was imminent gradually filtered through to the work force.

One night as I was washing down the mini-bin at finishing time, the Bear came over and said excitedly "The redundancy notices are in the post, Jock!"

"It had to come sooner or later." I said matter-of-factly.

His eyebrows shot up "Aren't you worried about it?"

I kept on hosing the wagon "Not a bit!"

The Bear went on "They say that the new firm is going to take on seventy five per cent of the existing staff."

"Well at least that's something."

He pressed on regardless "If they offer you a job Jock, will you take it?"

"No!"

He was getting agitated and curious "Bloody hell Jock, do you prefer the dole?"

I turned off the water "No, I've got a job to go to."

Surprise replaced his agitation as he asked "What is it?"

Rolling up the hose in a neat coil, I replied with a smile "Public relations officer with a local firm."

The Bear's eyebrows took partners for the last waltz "Public relations! Good grief Jock! What do you know about that?"

I could almost smell old Tom's pipe as I replied "Quite a lot! You see — I was taught by an expert!!"

OTHER TITLES FROM

Local History

Birkenhead Priory	£1.80
The Spire is Rising	£1.95
The Search for Old Wirral	£9.95
Birkenhead Park	£1.40
A Guide to Merseyside's Industrial Past	£1.95
Neston and Parkgate	£2.00
Scotland Road	£5.95
Helen Forrester Walk	£1.00
Women at War	£2.95
Merseyside Moggies	£1.00
Dream Palaces	£7.50

Local Shipping Titles

Sail on the Mersey	£1.95
The Mersey at Work — Ferries	£1.40
Ghost Ships on the Mersey	£1.40
The Liners of Liverpool – *Part I*	£2.95
The Liners of Liverpool – *Part II*	£2.95

Local Railway Titles

Seventeen Stations to Dingle	£2.95
The Line Beneath the Liners	£2.95
Steel Wheels to Deeside	£2.95
Seaport to Seaside	£4.25
Northern Rail Heritage	£1.95
A Portrait of Wirral's Railways	£3.95

History with Humour

The One-Eyed City	£2.95
Hard Knocks	£3.95

Other Titles

Speak through the Earthquake, Wind & Fire	£3.95
It's Me, O Lord	£0.40
Companion to the Fylde	£1.75
Bird Watching in Cheshire	£3.95